D1316922

What a Horse!

Several of the horses in the pasture were ambling in the direction of the fence, where the campers stood. Libby and Lynda immediately ducked between the rails and went to meet them. Libby stood on tiptoe to fling her arms around Foxy's neck, and Lynda headed for the big dapple gray, saying softly, "Hey, Dan! Long time no see!"

As Pam greeted each horse by name and encouraged the other girls to pat them, Emily stood very still and held her breath. Joker, the palomino, had stopped several feet from the fence. He stood there, switching his silvery tail and gazing at the girls through his big, velvety brown eyes. He was so beautiful—just like Emily's favorite model horse, the one she'd named Golden Boy.

If he comes over to me, that'll be a sign, Emily thought. *It'll be a sign that he's supposed to be my horse.* She didn't even want to think about what it would mean if he came over to Caro instead. Out of the corner of her eye she could see Caro staring at Joker, too.

Choose me! Choose me! Emily begged silently, concentrating with all her might.

HORSEBACK SUMMER
by Virginia Vail

Illustrated by Daniel Bodé

Troll Associates

Library of Congress Cataloging-in-Publication Data

Vail, Virginia.
    Horseback summer / by Virginia Vail; illustrated by Daniel Bode.
        p.   cm.—(Horse crazy ; #1)
    Summary: While spending the summer at a horse camp, Emily must
fight to keep spoiled Caro Lescaux from taking the horse Emily loves.
    ISBN 0-8167-1625-0 (lib. bdg.)   ISBN 0-8167-1626-9 (pbk.)
    [1. Camps—Fiction. 2. Horses—Fiction. 3. Friendship—Fiction.]
I. Bode, Daniel, ill. II. Title. III. Series: Vail, Virginia.
Horse crazy ; #1.
PZ7.V192Hor 1990
[Fic]—dc19   89-30583

A TROLL BOOK, published by Troll Associates,
Mahwah, NJ 07430

Copyright © 1990 by Troll Associates, Mahwah, New Jersey

All rights reserved. No part of this book may be used or
reproduced in any manner whatsoever without written
permission from the publisher.

Printed in the United States of America.

10 9 8 7 6 5 4 3 2 1

Chapter 1

"Okay, let's go over the list one more time. I want to make sure I have absolutely everything I'm going to need for camp." Emily Jordan handed a sheet of paper to her best friend, Judy Bradford, and kneeled on the floor next to her metal camp trunk. A lock of short brown hair fell over her forehead as she lifted the lid and sat back on her heels, admiring the neatly arranged clothing inside.

"Oh, Emily, gimme a break!" Judy groaned. "You're so organized, you make me sick! I haven't even begun to pack, and you've been ready for *weeks!* You must know every single sock by now."

"For your information, smarty, I didn't pack any single socks—only pairs," Emily said with a grin. "Has your mother finished sewing in your name tags yet?"

"Almost. She only has to do my pajamas and un-

1

derwear. When she's done, I'll start packing." Judy looked more closely at the list in her hand. "What's this weird brown splotch next to 'personal accessories'? Looks like peanut butter."

"It *is* peanut butter," Emily admitted. "I was checking out a couple of things the other day while I was having a sandwich, and some of the peanut butter must've escaped. C'mon, Judy—read."

Judy flopped onto her stomach on Emily's bed. "Okay, here goes. One heavy sweater . . ."

"Check."

"One hard hat . . ."

"Check."

"Three pairs of shorts . . ."

"Check."

"Two pairs of jeans and two pairs of breeches . . ."

"Check, check." Emily's gray eyes lit up as she carefully smoothed the riding pants. "Imagine, Judy! Day after tomorrow we'll be on our way to Webster's Country Horse Camp! I can hardly believe it. Do you suppose we'll be able to ride as soon as we get there?"

"I don't know, but it would be neat if we could. I wonder if we'll be able to choose our horses, or if the Websters will just assign a horse to each girl. I hope I don't get some old nag that's ready for the glue factory!"

Emily shuddered. "Judy! What a horrible thing to say! They don't make glue out of horses anymore.

Anyway, I'm sure Webster's horses are absolutely wonderful. You saw the pictures in the brochure. The horses were beautiful."

"All horses are beautiful," Judy agreed. "All I meant was, I'm not such a great rider, and maybe they'll give me a really slow, old horse. I'll never learn to be a better rider if I don't have a chance to handle a horse with some spirit."

"I know what you mean," Emily said. "Whenever we ride at The Barn, you get stuck with Frosty, and he isn't exactly a ball of fire."

Judy giggled. "Tell me about it! I love old Frosty, but I think he goes over all those trails in his sleep. When we get to Webster's, I'm going to learn to jump, and ride bareback, and everything!"

"Me, too," Emily agreed dreamily. "I'm looking forward to those overnight trail rides. Won't it be fun, riding our very own horses through the woods and camping out?"

For a moment, both girls were lost in visions of what they were sure was going to be the best summer of their whole lives. They'd been planning their summer at Webster's Country Horse Camp for almost an entire year. It hardly seemed possible that in just two days, their dream would come true. And one of the best parts about going to Webster's was that they were going together. Emily and Judy had been best friends forever—or at least for ten years, ever since they were three. They had gone to kindergarten and elementary school together, had chicken pox together, studied together, and played together. This past fall, they had entered junior high, where they were in the same homeroom. They were both horse crazy, and they hung out at the local riding stable, The Barn, almost every weekend, riding and helping to care for the horses. And now they were going to horse camp together.

"It's going to be so neat," Emily said with a happy sigh, closing the lid of her trunk. "I don't know how I'm going to stand waiting till day after tomorrow."

"Me, neither," Judy said. She bounced off Emily's bed. "But the way to make the time go faster is to keep busy every minute. So let's think of things to do. How about biking out to The Barn to say goodbye to Frosty and Pancho?" Pancho was the horse Emily always rode.

Emily shook her head, reluctant to part with her horse. "No—let's wait and do that tomorrow. Then we'll have more time. We don't just want to pay them a short visit when we're going to be gone so long, and if we go now, we'll have to be back home for supper—"

"Hey, Judy! Your mom's on the phone!" Emily's fifteen-year-old brother Eric yelled from downstairs.

"Rats!" Judy groaned. "I completely forgot I told Mom I'd help sew name tags this afternoon. I bet she's calling to remind me."

Emily followed her friend out of the room. "You better go and do it then. Call me tonight, okay?

5

We'll decide when we're going to The Barn tomorrow. I'll bring lots of carrots."

"And I'll bring apples. No sugar—it's bad for horses' teeth."

Judy dashed down the stairs and grabbed the phone from Eric. "Mom? Hi—it's me. What's up? Oh, no! Don't call the fire department—I'll be home in a few minutes. Don't panic, Mom. Everything'll be okay. Bye!" She hung up the phone.

Emily and Eric stared at her.

"Is your house on fire?" Eric asked.

"What's happened?" Emily asked.

"It's my kitten, Sprinkles. He's stuck way up in the maple tree in our backyard—that's why Mom was going to call the fire department. But we don't need a hook and ladder, because I can climb up and rescue him in a jiffy."

Judy ran for the front door, and Emily shouted after her, "Call me when you get him down!"

The door slammed behind Judy, and Eric shook his head. "Women! Just because some dumb cat gets stuck in a tree, they call the fire department." He went back into the living room, where he had been watching one of his favorite TV shows.

As Emily walked back to her room, she thought about Judy and how fond she was of her little black-and-white kitten. If anyone could get Sprinkles down from the tree, Judy could. That was one of the things she admired most about Judy—nothing ever fazed her. If it had been Emily's kitten, she had to admit that she'd have called the fire department, too—heights made her dizzy. But Judy was a daredevil. Feisty little blond Judy wasn't scared of anything! Judy would get Sprinkles down safe and sound, Emily was sure.

Judy didn't call until around eight o'clock that night, and when she did, her voice sounded strange.

"Hi, Emily. Uh . . . guess what?"

"What?" Emily asked anxiously. "Sprinkles is all right, isn't he?"

"Oh, yeah. He's fine. He was pretty scared, but I got him down okay. . . ."

"Judy? Something's wrong, isn't it?"

"Well, kind of." There was a long pause. "Emily, you'll never guess where I'm calling from."

"Where?"

"Well . . . I'm kind of in the hospital."

"The *hospital?!*" Emily gasped.

"Yeah—Ferris Memorial. I'm in a semi-private room, because . . . well . . ."

"Judy, *tell me!*"

Another long pause. "Uh . . . I kind of . . . fell out of the tree."

"*Judy!*"

". . . and I kind of broke my leg. In two places. But Sprinkles is just fine."

"You're kidding!"

"I'm not kidding, Emily." Judy sounded on the verge of tears. "So I won't be able to go to Webster's with you. I won't be able to do much of anything at all for a while. Not for a long time. So I guess—"

"I'm not going without you!" Emily interrupted, her own voice faltering. "No way am I going to horse camp without you!"

"That's dumb. C'mon, Emily, we've been looking forward to going to Webster's for *ages*. You *have* to go! If you don't I'll spend the rest of the summer feeling just horrible because I ruined your summer as well as mine. You *have* to go, and write to me about everything you do, or I'll turn into an absolute *blob!* You're going to go to Webster's, and you're going to say good-bye to Frosty for me, and you're going to have to have a good time for *both* of us, because if you don't, I'll be absolutely miserable!"

Emily swallowed once or twice until her voice returned to normal. "But we've always done everything together," she said. "It won't be any fun without you."

"Yes, it will. It'll be lots of fun . . . for me, too—kind of—when you write and tell me everything you're doing. And you can send me pictures of your horse, and the other girls, and everything. It'll be like I was there, too. And you don't really want to sit around all summer drawing pictures on my cast, do you?"

"Well . . ." When Judy put it that way, Emily couldn't honestly say she did. Still, Judy was her

8

very best friend in all the world. How could she leave her alone for six whole weeks?

"Emily, if you had broken *your* leg, *I'd* go," Judy continued. "I'd miss you, but I'd go. Otherwise, my folks would lose the deposit they paid when I registered. And your folks will, too, if you don't go."

Emily hadn't considered that. "I'll think about it," she said at last. "How long are you going to be in the hospital? Can I come and see you tomorrow?"

"The hospital?" said her mother, who had just entered the hall. "Who's in the hospital?"

"Judy. I'll tell you about it in a minute," Emily said, covering the mouthpiece. Then she turned back to the receiver.

"I'm going home early tomorrow," Judy told her. "I'll probably be home around ten. So come over, okay? A nurse just came in with some juice and pills and stuff. Gotta go. Bye!"

Still a little stunned, Emily hung up the phone to find her mother, her father, and Eric standing there, looking anxious.

"Why is Judy in the hospital?" they all asked at once.

Emily told them about Judy falling out of the tree while she was rescuing Sprinkles, and ended by saying, "So she's not going to Webster's, and now I don't want to go either. Judy says I should, but I don't want to, not without her. It won't be the same."

They had all ended up in the kitchen, and Mrs.

9

Jordan was pouring milk to go with the cookies she'd baked that afternoon. Emily sipped at her milk and took a bite of a chocolate chip cookie, but it tasted like sawdust.

"If you don't go, Mom and Dad will lose their deposit," Eric said, wolfing down three cookies.

"That's what Judy said," Emily sighed, handing the rest of her cookie to Eric.

"The money's not important," Mr. Jordan said. "What *is* important is how you feel, Emily."

"I think you oughta go," Eric said through a mouthful of cookie. "If you stay home, it's not going to make Judy's leg heal any faster."

"I know." Emily stared down at her milk. "But I've never done anything without Judy. What if I mess up? What if I'm the worst rider in the whole camp? What if none of the other girls like me? What if . . . ?"

"Honey, maybe it's time you did something all by yourself," Mrs. Jordan said, reaching out to touch Emily's hand. "I'm terribly sorry about Judy's accident, but you've been looking forward to going to Webster's for so long. Why don't you give it a try? If you don't like it, you can come home after two weeks. I think it's time you branched out on your own."

"I have to think about it," Emily said, draining her glass of milk. "Now I guess I better go to bed. Tomorrow's going to be a busy day, visiting Judy and saying good-bye to the horses at The Barn—if I decide to go to Webster's, that is."

After she had brushed her teeth, showered, put on her shortie pajamas and was snuggled up in bed, Emily was still filled with doubts. This summer at Webster's was supposed to be shared with Judy. If Judy wasn't going to be there, everything would be different. It had always been Judy who led the way, Judy who'd taken charge. Emily had always relied on Judy to be the first to make new friends and to plunge into new activities. If she went to Webster's alone, there would be no one to rely on but herself. She was sure the other campers would be much better riders than she was—much better at *everything*. Even surrounded by her beloved horses, even with a horse she could call her own for the whole summer, how would she cope?

Emily finally fell asleep, but her dreams were far from sweet. She dreamed she was surrounded by girls on beautiful horses. They were all watching as she tumbled time and again from the saddle of the biggest horse she'd ever seen. The girls were laughing at her, but the worst part was that the horses were laughing, too!

Chapter 2

"Well, here we are!" Mr. Jordan said a little too heartily as he slowed the family car and peered up at a sign by the side of the road. "Webster's Country Horse Camp—one mile. This must be the place."

"Guess so," Emily said in a small voice. Suddenly the four-hour drive seemed all too short. Maybe if they had another four hours to go, she'd be prepared. As it was, her stomach was doing flip-flops from nervousness—and yes, excitement. She hoped she wasn't going to throw up.

"You're not feeling carsick are you, honey?" her mother asked anxiously, noticing the look on Emily's face. "Want a mint?" She handed a roll of Life Savers over the front seat to Emily.

"Of course not, Mom," Emily said, but she took a mint anyway. "I stopped getting carsick ages ago. I just feel a little—funny, that's all."

"You'll be fine as soon as you get out of the car and stretch your legs," her father assured her, turning onto a narrow dirt road. The road was very bumpy, which didn't make Emily's stomach feel any better.

"It's been years since we've been to the Adirondacks," Mrs. Jordan said. "I'd forgotten how beautiful it is up here. All those lovely mountains towering over the farmland. And look, Emily! That must be the Winnepac River, where you'll be canoeing and boating. Isn't there a boys' camp on the other side? Longview or something?"

"Long Branch," Emily corrected. She looked out the window, too. Across the Winnepac, she could dimly see a cluster of cabins among the trees, and a flag fluttering in the breeze at the end of a dock.

"That's right, Long Branch. My, what a perfect location for a summer camp! I wouldn't mind spending the summer here myself," her mother said enthusiastically.

"Sorry, Meg—they don't take anyone over sixteen at Webster's," Mr. Jordan teased. "Guess you'll be stuck with Eric and me back home in Woodbridge."

Suddenly Emily wished she could trade places with her mother. Mom was like Judy—she fit in anywhere and made friends easily. Emily was quiet in the backseat, feeling more and more miserable, and thinking her mother would have a better time at

Webster's than she would. Then she looked out the window and saw the horse.

He was running in a field by the side of the road. He was a chestnut, and his deep mahogany coat seemed to glow in the sunlight as he galloped, mane and tail streaming behind him. Emily caught her breath.

"He's racing us, Dad!" she cried, leaning out the open window. "Look at him! Isn't he gorgeous?"

"If he's racing us, he's going to win, because I can't go more than ten miles an hour on this road," her father said as they hit another bump. The jolt didn't faze Emily in the least, although she almost swallowed what was left of her Life Saver.

"I bet he's one of Webster's horses," she said excitedly. "I wonder if all their horses are as beautiful as he is! I mean, like Judy said, *all* horses are beautiful, and I'll love whatever horse I get, but I hope my horse looks something like that. He doesn't have to be a chestnut, of course. Pancho back at The Barn is a fat old pinto, but I love him just the same. I wonder if he'll miss me. . . ." Emily rambled on as Mr. and Mrs. Jordan shared relieved smiles in the front seat.

"At Webster's, I'll be riding the same horse for eight weeks. A horse really gets to know you when you ride him and care for him for such a long time. Oh, wow, look at *that!*"

The chestnut had suddenly started bucking and kicking up his heels like a high-spirited colt, and

14

Emily laughed in delight. She didn't see the glance that passed between her mother and father as they silently agreed that their daughter was going to have the summer of her life.

But a few hours later, as Emily stood in the cabin she was to share with six other girls (it would have been seven if Judy had come), her excitement began to fade. She was the first of "The Fillies"—campers aged twelve to fourteen—to arrive. Her parents had stayed just long enough to complete her official registration with Marie Webster, who ran the camp with her husband, Matt. Then they had escorted Emily to the Fillies' cabin, given her lots of hugs and kisses, and taken off for their return trip to Woodbridge.

Webster's was *not* like Camp Canadion, the only other camp Emily had ever gone to before. Canadion, right outside of Woodbridge, was filled with kids Emily and Judy had gone to school with all their lives. If you had a problem, you could call your parents and you knew they could be there in about half an hour if the problem was really serious. And as with everything else they did, Emily and Judy had gone there together.

Webster's was altogether different. It wasn't just a jumble of cabins with a recreation hall used mainly for camper meals and rainy-day arts and crafts projects. Webster's was a real farm, with a farmhouse in which the Webster family lived.

15

Behind the farmhouse was a smaller building which housed "The Foals," younger girls aged eight through eleven. "The Thoroughbreds," the fifteen- and sixteen-year-olds, occupied a bunkhouse next to the Fillies' cabin. Emily had seen several Thoroughbreds go by, and she thought they looked awfully grown up. And the few Foals she'd seen looked awfully young. But, so far, she hadn't seen a single other Filly. The only person she'd met who seemed to be around her age was Chris Webster. He had dashed to the Jordans' car the moment it stopped under the big old elm trees in front of the farmhouse, flung open the door for Emily's mother, and said cheerfully, "Welcome to Webster's!"

Emily couldn't help being impressed by how relaxed and friendly he was with a carful of strangers, but she guessed he was used to meeting new campers and their families. It hadn't occurred to her that there might be boys at Webster's—the brochure had mentioned Pam Webster, who was the Fillies' counselor, and of course Matt and Marie Webster, who owned and ran the camp, but the only reference to the rest of the Webster family had been very vague. Emily could just hear Judy saying, "Hey, he's really cute!" She'd probably have said it so loud that Chris would have heard, and Emily would have been terribly embarrassed. But not Judy. Nothing ever embarrassed Judy.

It was Chris who had taken Emily's camp trunk and led the way to the Fillies' bunkhouse. He set the trunk down very carefully in the middle of the big room, saying, "Since you're the first one here, you have your choice of bunks. I wouldn't take the one in the corner if I were you—the top one sags, and the bottom one's hard as a rock."

"Thanks for the warning," Emily said. A moment later, he was gone, jogging off in the direction of the farmhouse.

So now Emily was all by herself, feeling very lonely and at loose ends. If only Judy were here! It would be fun checking out the bunks and settling in together. But since she was on her own, Emily knew she'd have to make the best of it.

She wandered around the room, poking gingerly at the mattresses on each lower bunk—she was afraid she might fall out of an upper bunk if she had to go to the bathroom or get up in the middle of the night and forgot where she was.

The bathroom! At Canadion, the cabins hadn't had individual bathrooms. Everybody had to walk down a little path to a special building where the facilities were located. Emily had hated that. So she looked around the bunkhouse and discovered to her relief that it had a bathroom. Thank goodness!

Having decided at last on the bunk she wanted, Emily was just dragging her trunk across the floor, when the front door burst open and a small, lively red-haired girl entered, followed by Chris, who carried a trunk very much like Emily's. Only this trunk was painted bright pink, dented in several places, and covered with brilliantly colored stickers.

"Hi!" chirped the new arrival, grinning at Emily. Her face was liberally sprinkled with freckles, her red hair stood on end, and she was wearing an over-sized T-shirt, patched jeans, and scuffed high-top sneakers. "I'm Libby Dexter. You're Emily—Chris told me. Hey, we're gonna be bunkmates! I always take the top one next to the window—or at least, I did last year."

Chris put Libby's trunk next to Emily's and left.

"Did you bring any posters?" Libby asked eagerly.

"Uh . . . posters?" Emily echoed. "What kind of posters?"

"You know—horses, rock stars, stuff like that. We gotta do *something* to decorate this place, or else it will look like a prison cell."

Libby dropped to her knees and opened her trunk, pulling out several rolled up posters. She unfurled one, revealing a life-sized picture of Michael J. Fox. "He's my passion," she told Emily, beaming. "Wherever I go, Michael goes with me. I'm gonna put him up right over my bed."

She scrambled up into the top bunk, then peered down at Emily. "Got any thumb tacks?"

"Uh . . . no, I'm afraid I don't," Emily said.

"No big deal. Dig around in my trunk—I have a roll of Scotch tape somewhere."

Emily obediently rummaged through the contents of Libby's trunk. Under a pile of mismatched socks she found the roll of tape. "Here you go," she said, tossing it up to Libby.

"You're just gonna love it here," Libby said as she taped the poster to the wall. "Webster's is absolutely, without a doubt, the greatest camp in the world. I've been coming here since I was eight. The Websters are like my own family." She sat back on her heels, admiring the result of her work. Then she leaped from the upper bunk, landing as gracefully as a cat on her feet next to Emily. "How good a rider are you?" she asked.

"Well, not very. I mean, I've never exactly had lessons or anything. I've been riding a lot the last few years," Emily told her, "but I'm not a very experienced rider."

"By the end of the summer you will be," Libby promised. "Matt's a super teacher. I didn't know one end of a horse from the other when I first came here, and now I want to be a jockey—if I don't grow too much taller, that is. But I don't think I will. My whole family's short. I'm really lucky, coming from a short family. You're pretty tall, though. You don't want to be a jockey, do you?"

"Oh, no," Emily said. "I just love horses, that's all. That's why I came to Webster's."

"I'm glad you don't want to be a jockey. You'd never make it, as big as you are." Libby clapped her hands over her mouth. "Hey, that didn't come out right! I don't mean you're *fat* or anything, just that

19

you're taller than I am. All my friends are taller than me, but I don't mind. And we're gonna be friends, Emily, real good friends, I can tell. I like you."

"I—I like you, too," Emily faltered shyly. And she did. She liked Libby a lot. If Judy were here, she'd like Libby, too, Emily was sure. Judy and Libby were a lot alike—bouncy and bubbly, like ice-cold ginger ale on a hot summer day. The girls grinned at each other, and suddenly Emily didn't feel lonely at all.

"Make way for more Fillies!" Chris Webster announced, clumping into the cabin with yet another trunk. Close on his heels came a tall, rosy-cheeked girl wearing shorts and a faded T-shirt with a picture of a horse on it.

"Lynda!" Libby yelled, scooting around Emily and giving the new girl a big hug. "You made it!"

"Of course I made it," Lynda said, laughing. "It wouldn't be summer if I didn't come to Webster's." Disentangling herself from Libby, she stuck out a hand to Emily. "Hi! I'm Lynda Graves. Who are you?"

Before Emily could reply, Libby said, "She's Emily . . . Emily what? I never did find out your last name."

"Emily Jordan," Emily said, shaking Lynda's hand. "This is my first summer at Webster's—but I guess you know that, if you've been coming here for a while."

"Since I was ten," Lynda told her. She dragged her trunk over to the bunk next to Emily's, opened it, and started taking out lots of pictures of horses. While the two old friends chattered, Lynda scrambled into the upper bunk and began tacking her pictures on the wall in a haphazard fashion. One picture in particular caught Emily's eye because it was different from all the others.

"A *cow?*" she asked.

"That's Bluebell, my heifer," Lynda said proudly. "She was my Four-H project this year, and we won first prize in the show this spring."

"Lynda's a farm girl," Libby told Emily. "All the way from Iowa." She grinned at Lynda. "Hayseed!"

Lynda grinned back. "Shrimp!" She turned to Emily. "Don't mind us. We have fun insulting each other."

At that point, things began to get pretty frantic in the Fillies' cabin, as three other girls arrived, all at the same time. Their camp trunks were delivered by Chris and an older boy Emily hadn't seen before. The second boy looked to be about sixteen or seventeen. He was tall and lean, with longish brown hair. If Chris was cute, this boy was positively handsome, Emily thought.

"That's Warren Webster," Lynda told her, climbing down from her bunk. "He's real cool, and he knows it. All the girls are crazy about him, even the Foals, but don't get any ideas—he's going steady with Melinda, the Foals' counselor."

Emily nodded, more interested in the girls who would be her cabin mates for the next six weeks

21

than in Warren Webster. As introductions were made all around, she found out that the quiet, blue-eyed blonde with pigtails was Penny Marshall, and the plump, scared-looking girl with braces was Drucilla something—Emily didn't catch her last name. The third girl, Danielle Franciscus, was absolutely beautiful, Emily thought. Her cloud of dark hair and olive complexion made her look very exotic and vaguely foreign somehow. Her dazzling smile was warm and friendly, and she didn't seem at all stuck-up, the way Emily always kind of expected very beautiful girls to be. Danielle immediately told everyone to call her Danny. One of the first things she unpacked was a very worn copy of *National Velvet,* which she tucked under the pillow of her bunk, saying, "This is my favorite book in all the world. I must have read it at least four times."

"Oh, me too!" Emily cried impulsively. "My brother gave me a tape of the movie for my birthday last year. I play it all the time on the VCR. Only I wish The Pi was a piebald in the movie, the way he was in the book, instead of making him a bay and calling him Pirate."

Danny made a face. "Yeah, I know. But the rest of it is so great. I have the tape, too. I used to rent it so often that my folks finally figured it would be cheaper to buy it!"

Now Emily decided it was time to start unpacking her own trunk. She hadn't been sure if campers were allowed to bring things to decorate their areas, but she'd tucked in photos of her family and three of her favorite model horses, just in case. She taped the snapshots of her parents and her brother over her bunk, which led Lynda to say, "Hey, who's that cool guy? Is he your boyfriend?"

Giggling, Emily said, "You mean Eric? No, he's my brother—my *older* brother." She couldn't wait to write to Eric and tell him that one of her cabin mates thought he was "cool." He'd get a kick out of that!

Her model horses also created quite a stir among Libby, Lynda, and Danny when she perched them on the little ledge at the head of her bunk. She just hoped they wouldn't fall down on her head in the middle of the night.

Absorbed as she was, Emily didn't notice right away that Penny and Drucilla were awfully quiet. But when she finally had her space arranged to her satisfaction, she glanced across the room and saw them sitting side by side on the lower bunk that Drucilla had chosen. They weren't saying a word to each other. They just sat there, looking glum. In fact, Drucilla seemed close to tears.

All of a sudden, Emily felt guilty. She and the other three girls had been ignoring Penny and Drucilla, and she knew they felt left out, just the way she would have felt without Judy if Libby, Lynda, and Danny hadn't been so friendly and warm. What would Judy do if she were here? Emily asked herself. She knew the answer. Judy would include them by going over and talking to them and making them

23

feel at home. So she marched over to Drucilla's bunk.

"This is my first summer at Webster's," she said. "What about you? Have you ever been to sleep-away camp before?"

Drucilla only shook her head.

"Uh . . . Drucilla, what do your friends call you? At home, I mean."

Drucilla mumbled something that Emily couldn't understand.

"Dru. They call her Dru," Penny volunteered, raising her round blue eyes to Emily. "She doesn't like to talk much, on account of her braces."

"Oh," Emily said. Then, "Hey, my brother Eric had braces for a while. At first they hurt so much that he couldn't eat anything but soup, but then it got a lot better. Now his teeth are just beautiful!"

Still, Dru didn't say anything. Emily was beginning to feel uncomfortable, as though she was bullying this fat, unhappy-looking girl. Why had Drucilla come to Webster's, anyway? Emily wondered.

Penny answered her unspoken question. "Dru loves horses, but she's kind of scared of them. She's afraid she'll be the worst rider of all the Fillies."

Emily could understand that. She'd felt the same way earlier but for some reason she didn't feel that way now.

"I bet you won't be," she said to Dru's bowed head. "Maybe *I'll* be the worst rider. That's worried me a lot. But if I am, I'm going to learn to be a *better* rider. And I love horses, too."

At last, Dru raised her head, staring at Emily with moist eyes. "You don't have to be nice to me," Dru said. "But thanks anyway." Emily couldn't think of anything else to say, so she shrugged, smiled, and returned to her bunk.

A moment later, the door to the bunkhouse opened again, and a big, cheerful girl strode in, beaming at all the campers.

"Hi, gang! I'm Pam Webster, your counselor. Sorry I couldn't get here before, but I've been helping Mom and Dad up at the house. Hey, Libby, Lynda! How ya doing? And you're . . ." she turned to Emily.

"Emily Jordan."

"Hi, Emily. Which one is Danielle?"

Danny waved from her bunk.

"Great! And you guys have to be Drucilla and Penny, right?"

The girls nodded silently.

"Fantastic! Judy Bradford's not coming, so there will be one empty bunk for a while. That leaves Caroline Lescaux. She ought to be here any minute now—oh, hi, Caro! Welcome to the Fillies' bunkhouse," Pam said as the door opened once again and a slender, blond girl stepped into the cabin.

Emily thought she looked like something out of a fashion magazine. She was wearing skin-tight jeans and a polo shirt with a little green alligator on

it. The blond girl glanced around at the bunks and their occupants, and said in ringing tones, *"This* is where I'm supposed to *sleep?* What is this—some kind of a joke?"

Uh-oh, Emily thought. *Here comes trouble!*

Chapter 3

Nobody said anything for what seemed like a very long time. Emily and the other five girls just stared at the newcomer. Even Pam Webster seemed at a loss for words at Caro's rudeness. The silence was broken by the entrance of Chris and Warren Webster, each staggering under the weight of several pieces of matching luggage, in addition to a camp trunk.

Chris dropped the suitcases he was carrying and said, "Whew! Guess you're planning to stay awhile, right?"

"Wrong!" Caro snapped. "You can just take my bags right out again. I'm going to find my father and tell him I can't possibly stay here."

"Oh, yeah?" Warren Webster said casually. "I hope you're fast on your feet. I just saw your dad's car heading down the road."

"Oh, no!" Caro wailed. For a minute, Emily thought the girl was going to burst into tears. Then she turned to Pam. "Look, there must be some mistake. I'm supposed to bunk with the Thoroughbreds. Daddy said he'd arrange it."

Pam smiled and shook her head. "I'm afraid not, Caro. The Thoros are fifteen and sixteen, and you're only fourteen. That makes you a Filly."

"But I'll be fifteen in October," Caro said. "I'm *much* older than these other girls. Why, those two . . ." she waved at Penny and Dru, who were still sitting side by side on Dru's bunk, solemnly staring at her, " . . . can't be more than *eleven!*"

"We're twelve," Penny said softly. "Going on thirteen. Both of us." Dru nodded.

"Can't you do something?" Caro pleaded with Pam. "I just know I'm going to be *miserable* here!"

"Sorry, Caro. I don't make the rules. Mom and Dad run the camp, and if they say you're a Filly, you're a Filly," Pam told her firmly.

Chris and Warren were edging out the door, but Caro suddenly grabbed Warren's arm before he could escape and gave him the most radiant smile Emily had ever seen. *"You* understand, don't you?" Caro said sweetly. "Can't you talk to your parents?"

"Hey, leave me out of this, okay?" Warren mumbled. Caro's smile faded like a lamp that had been switched off, and she let go of him. Warren beat a hasty retreat.

"Well, now, Caro," Pam said brightly, "why don't

29

you just take that bunk over there, the one in the corner? Top or bottom—your choice. One of the girls couldn't make it, so you can put some of your stuff on the bunk you decide not to use. Once you're settled in, I'll take you all on the grand tour and introduce you to the horses. Dad will assign your mounts tomorrow, right after breakfast, and Mom will post the roster so everybody knows what chores they'll be responsible for during the week. I have to check in with Melinda, the Foals' counselor, but I'll be back in about fifteen minutes. See you!"

With a cheerful wave, Pam departed.

"Chores?" Caro said. "What chores?"

"Didn't you read the brochure?" Lynda asked. "This isn't a country club, you know. We all get to help out on the farm while we're here." She grinned. "That's one of the reasons I like coming here so much—it's just like home, only it's a lot more fun."

"It doesn't sound like fun to me," Caro grumped, dragging her camp trunk over to the bunk in the corner. "It sounds like slave labor!"

"If you don't like anything about Webster's, then why did you come?" Libby asked as she picked up one of Caro's suitcases and put it next to the trunk.

Emily was wondering the same thing. Caro seemed to be the kind of girl who belonged at one of those fancy camps she'd read about, not a friendly family place like Webster's.

"It wasn't *my* idea," Caro said. "Mummy and

30

Daddy decided to send me here so I could 'broaden my horizons,' while they spend the summer in Europe. Of course, I've been to Europe several times, but I'd have liked to go with them just the same. . . ." Her voice sounded a little wistful, Emily thought, and for an instant she actually felt sorry for Caro. But the next moment, Caro's tone was as unpleasant as before. "I only hope this camp has some halfway decent horses," she said. "I'm not used to riding tired old plugs."

"Webster's has fantastic horses!" Libby said hotly. "And Matt Webster is a real pro. He used to train and ride champion jumpers on the international horse show circuit before he started this camp. He's a great riding teacher, too. And he and Marie are just about the nicest people in the world!"

Caro just shrugged and began unpacking her suitcases and her trunk. Since her bunk was next to the only clothes rack in the cabin, she immediately adopted the entire rack for herself. Emily was impressed by her wardrobe. Caro seemed to have an outfit for every occasion—and not just riding clothes, either. There were sundresses and party dresses and skirts and blouses, and shoes to match everything. Emily wouldn't have been surprised if she'd pulled out a ball gown to add to the collection. Where did she think she was going to wear all that stuff? Emily glanced over at Libby, who rolled her eyes in comic despair. Libby obviously thought all those clothes were as silly as Emily did.

But Danny and Lynda were fascinated. They edged closer and closer, and their eyes got bigger and bigger.

"I've never seen so many clothes outside of a store," Lynda said admiringly. "Except in the McKay's catalog. My mom orders most of our things from there."

Caro arched one eyebrow. "Really? I guess that's okay for tools and overalls. *My* mother shops at Preston Eliot's."

"I can tell," Danny said, recognizing the name of one of the most exclusive stores in the country. Touching the fabric of a pale blue shirt, she exclaimed, "This is real silk!"

"You can borrow it some time, if you like," Caro said, holding the shirt up to Danny. "You're probably about my size."

"Gee, thanks!" Danny said.

By the time Pam returned, Caro had completely dazzled Lynda and Danny, while virtually ignoring Emily, Libby, Penny, and Dru. She'd apparently decided that of her six cabin mates, Danny and Lynda were the only ones worth cultivating. That was fine with Emily—girls like Caro always made her feel awkward and tongue-tied. Besides, the most important thing about Webster's wasn't Caro's wardrobe. The *really* important thing was the horses, and she was itching to meet each and every one.

"Okay, Fillies," Pam said, sticking her head in the cabin door. "Everybody ready to go?"

"I bet I could conduct the tour all by myself," Libby said, grinning. "And Lynda, too. We probably know almost as much about Webster's as you do, Pam!"

"I wouldn't be surprised," Pam said cheerfully. "Why don't you two take over, and I'll just tag along."

Lynda managed to tear herself away from Caro, and Danny followed. Caro hung up one last dress, then joined them. Emily looked over at Dru and Penny, who were still sitting on Dru's bunk, looking sad. "Coming?" she asked. The two younger girls stood up reluctantly. They reminded Emily of Tweedledum and Tweedledee in *Alice in Wonderland.* Well, at least they had each other. But Emily couldn't help feeling responsible for them somehow. "I can't wait to see the horses we're going to be riding," she said.

"Me, too," Penny said, trotting along beside Emily. "I like horses a lot." She smiled shyly. "I collect model horses like yours, but I didn't bring any of them. Now I wish I had."

Dru didn't say anything. She just moped along at Penny's side, her lips clamped tightly over her braces. She still looked as if she might start crying any minute. Emily wanted to give her a friendly poke and say, "Lighten up!" but she didn't. Judy would have, if she'd been there. But Emily just wasn't as good as Judy with things like that. Instead, she ran

33

up to Libby and Lynda, who were leading the way around the camp.

"That's the Thoros' bunkhouse, under that oak tree over there," Libby was saying. "How many Thoros are there this year, Pam?"

"Six—a full house," Pam Webster said. "And we have eight Foals in the cabin next to the house. Melinda will have her hands full this summer—she's the Foals' counselor, and she's also my brother Warren's girlfriend," she added, with a swift glance at Caro.

"Where are the horses?" Emily asked eagerly. "When we were coming down the road, I saw a beautiful chestnut running in the field, but he's the only horse I've seen so far."

Pam laughed. "That's Brandy. He used to be Dad's favorite mount, but now he's retired. Brandy's almost twenty years old."

Emily was amazed. "He looked lots younger!"

"That's because we take such good care of him," Pam told her. "He won a lot of prizes when he was jumping, but now he's earned a nice long rest."

Libby had sprinted ahead, and now she clambered up on a white rail fence surrounding a big pasture that sloped down to the river.

"These are the horses we'll be riding," she said over her shoulder. "See that reddish bay with the black mane and tail, and the black tips on his ears? That's Foxy—he's mine!" She turned to Pam. "He *is* mine this summer, isn't he? Matt hasn't assigned him to anyone else?"

"He's yours, all right," Pam said with a friendly smile. "Dad wouldn't dare give Foxy to anyone but you."

Emily leaned over the fence, gazing out at the horses and ponies grazing in the pasture. She picked out Foxy right away—he was the only reddish bay with black-tipped ears. But there were so many others! Blacks, and dark bays, a gray and a white, a few chestnuts like Brandy, a sorrel or two, a strawberry roan—and a palomino. Oh, that palomino! The late-afternoon sun gleamed on his golden coat and made his silver-white mane and tail shine like clouds in a summer sky. The palomino was the most beautiful horse Emily had ever seen. As she watched, the palomino tossed his head, then seemed to look right at her with his huge brown eyes. Emily's breath caught in her throat. He's *my* horse! she thought. He *has* to be my horse!

But that's impossible, she immediately decided. A horse like that will probably be assigned to a super rider—somebody who's had a lot more experience than I've had. Somebody like Caro, whose golden beauty would echo that of the horse. They'd be a perfect team. There was no way in the world he'd ever be given to Emily for a whole summer.

"There's Dandy!" Lynda cried. "See him? That gorgeous dapple gray? Can I ride him again this summer, Pam?"

35

"You bet!" Pam said. "It's all been taken care of."

"Fantastic!" Lynda sighed. "Dan's my boy. I've been riding him for years!"

"I want the palomino."

Caro's voice cut into Emily's reverie, and she almost cried out, "Oh, no!" But she didn't. She bit her lip very hard and said nothing.

"Joker? Well, I don't know, Caro," Pam said. "The only ones I'm sure of are the horses that previous campers like Libby and Lynda have always ridden. The rest of them are up for grabs, until Dad makes the assignments tomorrow. As I said before, I don't make the rules. Maybe you'll get Joker, and maybe you won't. Nobody knows but Dad, and he's not telling—not yet, anyway."

Caro scowled, and Emily's heart leapt. Maybe, just maybe . . .

"Are any of them real nice and quiet?" Dru asked in a small, worried voice. "I mean, *really* quiet? They all look so *big*. . . ."

"Oh, lots of them are as gentle as lambs," Pam assured her. "See that strawberry roan over there next to the big black gelding?"

Dru nodded, her eyes on the calm, slightly plump horse.

"That's Bella Donna," Libby put in. "Her name means 'beautiful lady' in Italian. I rode her the first year I came here—she's quiet as can be. I bet Matt will give Donna to you."

36

"Yes, she'd be perfect for you," Caro said much too sweetly. "You're both almost the same shape!"

What an awful thing for Caro to say, Emily thought. Caro just wasn't a very nice person at all. Emily wished there was some way Caro could be allowed to bunk with the Thoroughbreds. Maybe the older girls would be able to put her in her place.

"Caro, that was unkind," Pam said quietly. "I'm sure you didn't mean to hurt Dru's feelings—or Donna's, either," she added, smiling a little. "But since Donna couldn't hear you, I think it'll be okay if you only apologize to Dru."

Caro's pretty face flamed, and it looked as though she was about to protest, but then she tossed her head and said, "Sorry, Dru. I guess it's just what my mother calls puppy fat. I bet if you went on a real strict diet, you'd lose it in a few years."

If that wasn't exactly the sort of apology Pam had in mind, she didn't pursue the subject further. Instead, she put an arm around Dru's plump shoulders and said, "Look—the horses are coming over to say hello!"

Several of the horses in the pasture were ambling in the direction of the fence where the Fillies stood. Libby and Lynda immediately ducked between the rails and went to meet them. Libby stood on tiptoe to fling her arms around Foxy's neck, and Lynda headed for the big dapple gray, saying softly, "Hey, Dan! Long time no see!"

As Pam greeted each horse by name and encour-

37

aged the other girls to pat them, Emily stood very still and held her breath. Joker, the palomino, had stopped several feet from the fence. He stood there, switching his silvery tail and gazing at the girls out of his big, velvety brown eyes. He was so beautiful—just like Emily's favorite model horse, the one she'd named Golden Boy.

If he comes over to me, that'll be a sign, Emily thought. *It'll be a sign that he's supposed to be my horse.* She didn't even want to think about what it would mean if he went over to Caro instead. Out of the corner of her eye she could see Caro staring at Joker, too.

Choose me! Choose me! Emily begged silently, concentrating with all her might.

Suddenly, a chunky little bay sidled up to Joker and gave him a playful nip on the flank. Joker flung up his head and kicked his heels, then turned abruptly and cantered off after the bay.

"Okay, Fillies, time to continue the tour," Pam said. "We'll just have time to check out the stables and the barn, and make a quick trip to the river before supper. There's a big dinner bell over by the house. When Chris rings it, we'll hear it wherever we are."

As the rest of the girls hurried to keep up with Pam's long stride, Emily lagged behind, looking over her shoulder at the horses in the field. She saw only Joker. He was *her* horse, the horse of her dreams.

But she heard Caro saying to Danny, "The palo-

mino's the one I want. And I'll get him, too, just you wait and see."

Emily clenched her jaw. She'd never been a fighter, but if there was the slightest chance she could persuade Matt Webster to assign Joker to her, she'd fight like mad to prevent Caro from taking him from her.

"Wouldn't you just like to *kick* her?" Libby muttered, skipping along beside Emily. "She's so sure of herself, it makes me sick."

Emily looked down at the feisty little redhead and grinned. "Me, too!" she muttered back.

Chapter 4

The Fillies were down by the dock, peering across the Winnepac River at what they could see of the boys' camp, when they heard the dinner bell.

"Chow time!" Pam called. "I don't know about you, but I'm hungry enough to eat a . . ." she paused, then grinned at them all " . . . a *bear!*"

"I'm awfully glad she didn't say a horse," Danny giggled. "I don't think I'd ever be hungry enough for that!"

"I won't let my dad buy canned horsemeat for our dogs," Lynda said. "I can't imagine how anybody could turn a horse into pet food, no matter how old the horse was!"

Emily shuddered. "I don't even want to *think* about it!"

The girls trudged up the path leading from the river to the Websters' big old farmhouse, and joined the other campers as they filed into the dining room. Pam told them that it had once been two rooms, but they'd knocked down a wall to make it big enough to hold all of the Webster's campers at one time. There were four long tables with chairs on either side and one at each end. The tables were covered with bright blue-and-white checkered tablecloths, and in the center of each was a bouquet of wild-flowers. Emily thought it looked very cozy and homey, but Caro fingered a corner of one of the tablecloths and said with a sniff, "Plastic. Ugh!"

"Libby and Lynda will show you where to sit," Pam said. "I have to help serve. But starting tomorrow, you'll all be helping out." She waved and strode off to join her parents, her brothers, and the other counselors who were bringing platters of fried chicken and bowls of vegetables out of the kitchen and putting them on the tables.

"Meals are family-style at Webster's," Lynda said. "Marie cooks everything herself, and her meals are always great."

"You can sit anywhere you like," Libby added. "We don't have special tables for Foals, Fillies, and Thoros, but the groups usually wind up sitting together anyway."

Emily, Penny, and Dru followed Libby to the nearest table, but Caro grabbed Danny's arm and said, "Let's sit over there, with the older girls. Coming, Lynda?"

Lynda hesitated, then shrugged and said, "Why not?"

Caro, Danny, and Lynda squeezed onto a bench at a table where several Thoroughbreds were already seated. Lynda knew some of the girls from previous years, and began making introductions.

"I'm really surprised at Lynda," Libby told Emily, frowning. "I'd have thought she was too smart to fall for Caro's princess act, but I guess you never can tell."

Even though the food looked and smelled delicious, Emily wasn't very hungry. As the seats at their table quickly filled with an assortment of Foals and a Thoro or two, she suddenly felt very lonely. She wondered what Judy was doing right now. She would probably be out in the backyard in her cast playing with Sprinkles. Emily's folks would probably just be pulling up in front of their house, and Eric would have gotten home from his summer job at the supermarket a little while ago. Not even the thought of Joker could prevent her from feeling desperately homesick. Emily stared down at the golden-brown pieces of chicken on her plate, and at the vegetables and salad, unable to eat a bite.

"You're Emily Jordan, aren't you?"

Emily looked up to find that Marie Webster had taken the chair at the head of the table to her right. Marie was about Emily's mother's age, with short, curly blond hair and friendly blue eyes. She was wearing a faded plaid shirt and equally faded jeans.

"That's right," Emily said, trying to return Marie's warm smile.

"It's too bad about your friend—Judy Bradford, right?"

Emily nodded.

"I guess you must miss her a lot," Marie went on. "Your parents told me that the two of you have always done everything together. It's tough sometimes, being on your own. Makes you feel a little lost at first, doesn't it?"

Emily nodded again, swallowing a lump in her throat.

"I know exactly how you feel. The first time I went away to camp without my twin sister, I felt like half a person. But you know something, Emily? I found out that summer that I *wasn't* half a person—I was a *whole* person. Me. And I wouldn't be at all surprised if you started feeling that way, too, a lot sooner than you think."

It was as if Marie had read Emily's mind. Spooky, almost. The lump in Emily's throat began to dissolve, and she realized that she was hungry after all. Besides, she couldn't hurt Marie's feelings by not at least trying to eat the food she'd prepared.

"Thanks, Mrs. Webster," she said softly.

"Marie. Everybody calls us Matt and Marie."

"Okay—Marie." Emily picked up a chicken leg and took a bite. "This chicken is really delicious!"

Marie looked pleased. "Glad you like it. There's plenty more if you want seconds—or even thirds.

And if there's any left over, it's chicken salad tomorrow for lunch!"

Emily smiled. "I'm crazy about chicken salad."

As the campers were finishing their dessert—home-made shortcake, topped with home-grown strawberries and whipped cream—Matt Webster stood up and tapped a knife on his glass to get everyone's attention. He looked just like his picture in the brochure, Emily thought, tough and tanned and wiry, with a big, horsey smile just like Pam's.

"I want to welcome you all to Webster's, and tell you how glad Marie and I are to have you here," he began. "Hope you enjoyed your supper . . ."

Everybody applauded.

". . . but I want you to know that I had absolutely nothing to do with it. Marie's the kitchen magician, and she'll be teaching you some of her tricks when you take turns helping her prepare our meals from now on.

"As you all know by now, Webster's is different from other horse camps. When you come to Webster's, you become part of our family for the summer, and like the rest of our family, you'll be expected to do certain chores every day, in addition to riding and taking care of your horses. We've posted a duty roster on the bulletin board next to the kitchen door, and your counselors will make sure you know who does what on any given day. Incidentally, tonight it's the Fillies' turn to clean up after supper—'' Matt was interrupted by some loud groans from the Fillies. He laughed, then continued. ''Those of you who have been here before know that cleaning up is no big deal. We have two big dishwashers—all you have to do is scrape and stack.

''Now, I know that the main thing on everybody's mind is *horses*. Who's going to be assigned which horse? You'll find out tomorrow, after breakfast. And then the riding lessons, preparation for our horse shows, trail rides, and other good stuff begin. If you don't know how to take care of a horse, believe me, you'll learn. And you'll learn to ride safely and intelligently, and to consider your mount's welfare at all times.''

''If you have any problems or questions, Marie and I will be more than happy to help you. One or the other of us is always here. Now, if everybody's finished with their dessert, I'm going to ask the Fillies to clear the tables, and then you can all go back to your cabins, finish unpacking, write letters, whatever. There'll be a marshmallow roast and singalong in about an hour down by the river, and you're all cordially invited to attend. . . .'' He paused and looked over at Marie. ''Did I miss anything, honey?''

Marie laughed and said, ''Can't think of a thing.''

''Well, then, I guess that's the end of the speech. See you in about an hour.''

46

Everybody applauded again, and the general babble of conversation filled the big room.

Marie stood up and stretched. "Okay, Fillies," she said to Emily, Libby, Penny, and Dru, "let's start cleaning up." She turned to Libby. "How about reminding Lynda and her pals that they're included?"

"You bet!"

Libby went over to the table where Caro, Lynda, and Danny were sitting and tapped Lynda on the shoulder. "Clean-up time. You guys, too," she added pointedly to Danny and Caro. Lynda and Danny immediately began collecting the dessert plates, but Caro pretended she hadn't heard.

"*Caro!* Get with it," Libby snapped.

Caro stared up at her, then clapped a hand to her forehead. "Gee, Libby, I've got this *terrible* headache. It happens every time I eat strawberries. I shouldn't have had dessert, but it looked so good I just couldn't resist. Silly of me, but I'm sure you understand. I think I'd better go back to the cabin and lie down for awhile. I'll take a couple of aspirin, too. Excuse me, will you?"

"I just can't *believe* that girl!" Libby said as Caro hurried out of the dining room, still clutching her head. "Like my grandmother says, she gives me a pain that a pill can't cure!"

Emily giggled, juggling a tray stacked high with dessert dishes. "My grandmother says the very same thing! And now I know exactly what she means."

* * *

47

After the Fillies had done their chores, they returned to the bunkhouse, where Caro was lying on her bunk, a wet washcloth on her head. When Lynda put a Bruce Springsteen tape into her cassette player and turned the volume up, Caro groaned loudly, but Lynda didn't turn it down.

Emily curled up in her bunk and began a letter to Judy. There was so much to say, she was sure she'd never finish it before the marshmallow roast, but that was all right. She'd fill in the rest of the details tomorrow morning. She had just gotten to a description of Joker when Pam poked her head in the door and said, "Time for the campfire. C'mon, gang, let's go!"

Dru actually brightened up. "I love marshmallows," she said.

"So do I," Penny said, climbing out of her upper bunk. "We better bring sweaters or something—it's getting kind of cold."

Emily tucked her letter under her pillow and dug into her trunk for a sweatshirt. Libby, Lynda, and Danny hurriedly struggled into sweatshirts and sweaters, and Danny paused by Caro's bunk, saying, "Aren't you coming, Caro? Don't you feel better?"

Caro's long, golden eyelashes fluttered slightly. "A little. You go on. If I feel up to it, I'll come later."

Pam came into the cabin and went over to Caro. "Maybe you ought to let Mom take a look at you," she said. "She's a registered nurse, you know. If you

48

don't show up in about half an hour, I'm going to send her over, okay?"

Caro sighed deeply and opened one eye to gaze at Pam. "I'm sure I'll be all right by then. I don't want to be any trouble to anyone. . . ." Her voice trailed off into a whisper.

"That's the spirit!" Pam said heartily. Turning to the other girls, she added, "Follow me, Fillies!"

The sun was sinking into the woods on the opposite side of the river, dyeing the sky a brilliant orangy-red, when the Fillies joined the rest of the campers at the campfire site. But underneath the tall pine trees it was already dark as night. Warren and Chris were feeding logs into the blazing bonfire that banished the darkness with its glow, reflecting on the faces of the girls as they assembled around it. Emily sat down next to Libby, and Penny, Dru, and Danny joined them. Emily wondered what had happened to Lynda. Had she gone back to the cabin to take care of Caro?

"Where's Lynda?" she asked Libby, who shushed her, saying, "Just wait and see."

"Where are the marshmallows?" Dru asked plaintively.

"*Sssh!* You'll get plenty of marshmallows later," Libby said. "First comes the scary part."

"What scary part?" Penny asked, edging closer to Dru. "I don't like scary things!"

"It's just *pretend* scary, not *real* scary," Libby assured her. "It's fun. You'll like it, believe me."

49

From somewhere deep in the woods, an owl hooted, sending shivers up and down Emily's spine. She didn't like scary things, either. But Judy wasn't scared of anything. If only Judy were here. . .

Suddenly an eerie wail took up where the owl left off. It got louder and louder, and then the wail turned into words.

"Beware the Vipers! The Vipers are coming!" the voices wailed. The Foals clutched each other and squealed. Emily didn't squeal, but she wasn't exactly comfortable.

"The Vipers are coming! The Vipers are coming!"

The voices seemed to come from all around.

"Beware the Vipers!"

Shadowy figures draped in something pale and formless emerged from between the trees, moaning and waving their arms.

"The Vipers are coming! The Vipers are coming!"

By now, even the Thoroughbreds were shrieking and clutching each other. Dru reached out and grabbed Emily's arm, whimpering, "I want to go home!"

The dancing flames of the bonfire made everything look weird and spooky.

"The Vipers are coming! The Vipers are coming!"

A Foal shrieked and buried her head in her counselor's lap.

Then two figures trudged into the circle of light cast by the bonfire. They were wearing shapeless garments secured around the waist by aprons, and they held bunched-up rags in their hands.

"Ve're the vipers! Ve've come to vipe the vindows!" they shouted, leaping around and making wiping motions with their rags.

Everybody dissolved in laughter, fending off the attacks of the "vipers," who rubbed at their faces, giggling. Emily recognized Lynda as one of the "vipers," and gave Dru a shake.

"There's nothing to be scared of. See—it's Lynda!"

Dru managed a faint giggle, and Emily laughed as hard as Libby did when Lynda gave them both a swipe with her rag.

Then the "vipers" disappeared into the darkness and, having discarded their costumes, returned as Lynda and one of the Thoros.

"You were a great viper," Emily said, as Lynda hunkered down next to her. "You scared me to death!"

"Did I really? Gee, thanks! I've never been a viper before. The first time they pulled it on me, I was terrified out of my mind," Lynda said, grinning.

Matt stood up, raising his hands to calm down the excited laughter of the campers.

"I guarantee this is the scariest thing that's going to happen to you at Webster's. And now, let's sing a little. How about 'Witchcraft,' Warren?"

Warren Webster stepped out of the shadows, an acoustic guitar in his hands. He struck a chord and began to play the first notes of the song. Most of the campers seemed to know it, including Emily. She'd sung it with Judy at Camp Canadion.

"If there were witchcraft, I'd make three wishes,
     A wandering road that beckons me from home . . ."

And when the song was finished, Warren launched into "Riding on a Donkey":

"Hey, ho, up we go, donkey riding, donkey riding,
     Hey, ho, up we go, riding on a donkey!"

Then they sang "White Coral Bells," dividing into groups so it could be sung as a round. Emily loved "White Coral Bells"—it was her favorite camp song. Judy's, too, she thought with a pang.

As the song ended, and the last group's clear treble voices faded away into the night, mingling with the chirping of crickets and the far-off call of a loon, the figure of a girl floated out of the woods. At first, Emily thought it was part of another stunt, like the "vipers." But as the girl moved closer to the campfire, she recognized Caro, wearing a pale pink dress. The firelight glimmered on her golden hair, making her seem to be an apparition from another world.

"Doesn't Caro look *gorgeous?*" Danny sighed. "I'd give anything to be beautiful and blond like she is, and have all those lovely clothes!"

"Yeah," Lynda said softly. "I guess she's feeling better."

Apparently, Caro was. She drifted over to where Warren was standing, strumming random chords on his guitar, and smiled sweetly at him. "I'm so sorry I missed the first part of the sing-along. I had this terrific headache, but it's all gone now," she said. "You play really well. I just *love* the sound of a guitar!"

Warren stared at her as though he'd never seen her before. "Uh . . . thanks," he mumbled.

Libby nudged Emily sharply in the ribs. "Oh, brother!" she whispered. "Look at Princess Caroline!"

Now a slender girl with long auburn hair detached herself from the group of Foals and marched over to Warren and Caro.

"How about 'She'll Be Comin' Round the Mountain'?" she asked Warren, ignoring Caro. "The sing-along's not over yet, you know."

"That's Melinda Willis, Warren's girlfriend," Libby told Emily, grinning. "It'd be neat if she decked Caro right here and now!"

"She wouldn't really, would she?" Emily asked, her eyes widening.

Libby snorted. "Of course not! But it would be neat if she did."

" 'She'll Be Comin' Round the Mountain,' Warren," several voices called.

"Yeah, right," Warren called back, adjusting the shoulder strap of his guitar and turning away from Caro. "Here you go!"

Caro wandered over to where the rest of the Fillies were seated and sank gracefully onto the ground

next to Danny as Warren played the opening chords of the song. Everyone knew the words, even the youngest Foals, and they all sang at the top of their lungs:

"She'll be comin' round the mountain when she comes,
She'll be comin' round the mountain when she comes,
She'll be comin' round the mountain,
She'll be comin' round the mountain,
She'll be comin' round the mountain when she comes!"

"I *love* your dress, Caro," Lynda whispered between verses.

"Thanks," Caro whispered back. "You can borrow it sometime. I may even give it to you—it's old, and I have lots more."

Emily met Libby's eyes and stifled a giggle as Libby, who was sitting where Caro couldn't see her, clutched her throat with both hands and pretended to gag. Then Warren led the campers into another verse, and Emily sang lustily with the others:

"She'll be drivin' six white horses when she comes,
She'll be drivin' six white horses when she comes,
She'll be drivin' six white horses,
She'll be drivin' six white horses,
She'll be drivin' six white horses when she comes!"

That was Emily's favorite verse. She could just picture herself driving six white horses round the mountain.

"We will all run out to meet her when she comes,
    We will all run out to meet her when she
    comes . . ."

That night, when the Fillies climbed into their beds, a bloodcurdling scream from Caro's bunk made the rest of the girls sit bolt upright, bug-eyed. Someone had put a frog in her bed. Pam removed the frog and delivered a brief lecture on practical jokes. Nobody confessed, but Emily could feel her entire bunk quivering as Libby silently doubled up with muffled laughter.

Chapter 5

The next morning, Emily was so excited that she could hardly swallow the delicious scrambled eggs Marie had fixed for breakfast. In less than an hour, she'd know what horse had been assigned to her for the summer. Last night she'd dreamed about Joker—she'd been riding the beautiful palomino bareback, and Judy had been beside her, riding Foxy, Libby's horse. They'd been laughing and having a wonderful time.

Was it possible that Emily would be lucky enough to be given Joker? She was actually trembling when Pam led the Fillies—all wearing riding clothes and the velvet-covered hard hats that were required whenever the campers rode—to the stables where the assignments were posted. Emily was afraid to look at the list. If Joker had been assigned to someone else, she didn't think she could stand it!

"Okay, Fillies, listen up!" Pam announced. "Dr. Pepper will be Penny's horse. You're gonna love Pepper, Penny. Both your names begin with *P!* Pepper's a real sweetheart. You won't have any trouble with him. Dru, you'll be riding Donna. She has the nicest disposition of any horse we own."

Penny and Dru nodded solemnly in unison.

"Danny, you get Midnight Mist. She's a good, steady mare. We call her Misty for short."

Danny's eyes lit up. "Like 'Misty of Chincoteague'!" Then she asked anxiously, "She's not a pony, is she? I'd feel pretty silly riding a pony."

Pam laughed. "No, Misty's almost fifteen hands high. Only some of the Foals ride our ponies. Lynda, you'll be riding Dandy, and as I said yesterday, Dad wouldn't dare give Foxy to anybody but Libby."

"Cool!" Libby said, grinning, and Lynda grinned, too.

Emily's hands were clenched into fists. Her palms were sweaty. There were only two Fillies left—herself, and Caro. Would Joker be assigned to one of them?

"Caro's horse will be Dark Victory," Pam went on. "Vic for short. He's kind of a handful, Caro, but according to your questionnaire, you've had a lot of riding experience, so I'm sure you'll be able to control him."

"Dark Victory?" Caro said, pouting and swishing her riding crop against her custom-made breeches

58

and gleaming leather boots. "What about that palomino? He's the horse I really want."

"Oh, he's not enough of a challenge for a rider who's as advanced as you are," Pam said. "Joker's been assigned to Emily."

Emily felt as if she'd died and gone to horse heaven. She could hardly believe her ears. Her dream had come true! Joker was *her* horse!

Caro's pout turned into a scowl. If looks could kill, Emily was sure she'd have been dead on the spot, but she didn't care. In fact, she could almost feel sorry for Caro, losing out on a horse like Joker.

Then Caro tossed her blond head and said coolly, "Well, if Matt doesn't think Joker's good enough for me, I guess he must be right."

"Now that you all know the horses you'll be riding this summer, the first thing you do is bring them in from the pasture," Pam instructed. "After you lead them to their stalls, each of you will groom your mount, saddle him—or her—up, and head for the training ring. Riding classes begin in . . ." she consulted her watch ". . . forty-five minutes, Let's go, Fillies!"

As Pam strode off toward the pasture, Caro hurried along behind her. "We have to groom our own horses? I thought Chris and Warren would do that."

Pam glanced down at her. "Nope. That's part of the learning experience here at Webster's. A horse isn't a machine, like a fancy sports car you take for a spin, then drop off at the service station for a tune-

59

up. By caring for your horse, you establish a personal relationship with him. Horses are very sensitive animals. They respond to love just the way people do." She looked around at the rest of the Fillies, smiling. "And you all love horses, or you wouldn't be here, right?"

Everybody nodded, and Emily whispered, "Oh, yes!"

"I guess we also have to muck out their stalls," Caro grumbled. "I don't see what that has to do with love!"

"Don't you?" Pam asked in surprise. "Haven't you ever been sick, maybe even throwing up a lot, and your mother took care of you? You know, cleaned up the mess and put you into bed with nice clean sheets and made chicken broth for you to drink?"

"Oh, for goodness' sake!" Caro said irritably. "These horses aren't sick. And besides, my mother's always much too busy to do things like that for me—that's what she pays our housekeeper for."

Now Emily *did* feel sorry for Caro. Imagine your mother being too busy to care for you when you were sick! But she didn't have much time to think about it, because they'd reached the horse pasture and she could see Joker ambling toward the fence along with several of the other horses. He was every bit as beautiful as she remembered.

"And you're *mine*," she said softly as she ducked between the rails and walked to meet him, her hand outstretched. Emily wasn't aware of Pam urging Penny and Dru to find their mounts, or of her pointing out Dark Victory and Misty to Caro and Danny. She didn't notice Libby and Lynda briskly heading for their horses, or the Thoros and Foals being paired up with their mounts.

All she saw was Joker, standing there like a golden statue, gazing at her. It was almost as if he knew who she was, and he was waiting for her to come and claim him. Would he run away, the way he had yesterday, the first time she'd seen him?

He didn't. Instead, he stretched out his glossy neck and gently nudged her hand with his nose. Emily stroked him, feeling his satiny warmth beneath her hand. She slipped her arms around his neck and pressed her cheek against him, savoring his scent. Then she took hold of his halter and led him to the gate. She'd never felt so proud in her life. The most beautiful horse in the whole world, and he was *hers!*

Emily was glad she and Judy had spent so many hours at The Barn back home—Pam didn't have to tell her anything at all about how to groom Joker. His coat was in perfect condition, so all he really needed was a light brushing. His four white socks were a little muddy, so Emily found a soft-bristled brush in the tack room, dipped it in water, and carefully scrubbed each leg from the knee down. Then she rubbed him down from head to tail, using a soft, clean rag, until he gleamed like polished brass. As she worked, talking softly to him all the while, Joker stood patiently in his stall.

"Sorry, Joker," she said when she jerked the comb through his mane too hard and the horse turned his head to gaze at her reproachfully. "I'll try to be more gentle, because I know just how you feel. When I was little and my mother used to comb my hair, sometimes it felt like she was pulling it out by the roots, but she didn't mean to hurt me. And I don't mean to hurt *you*. I'll never hurt you, believe me!"

Caro's head popped up over the partition between Joker's stall and Vic's. Her hair was straggling around her flushed face, and there was a smudge on one cheek. "You act as though that horse could understand you," she said, brushing a strand of hair out of her eyes and leaving another smudge on her forehead. "You're weird, Emily! And anyway, horses have real thick hides. A little tweak won't hurt them."

"Some horses, maybe, but not Joker," Emily said, continuing to comb Joker's silvery mane. "He has tender skin, I can tell."

Resting her chin on the partition, Caro said grudgingly, "He looks pretty good. But then, I guess he wasn't very dirty. *This* one's absolutely *filthy!* Pam said he must have been rolling in the mud or something. She gave me a curry comb, and I've been currying him like mad, but he doesn't seem to be getting any cleaner, and *I'm* getting dirtier by the minute!"

Emily peered into Vic's stall. The big bay gelding was pawing the ground, and tossing his head the way Caro often did. His dark coat was still caked with dried mud in places, and he didn't look happy. Neither did Caro.

Just then, Pam, who had been showing Dru how to groom Donna, came over to Vic's stall. "How's it coming, Caro?" she asked cheerfully.

"Terrible!" Caro wailed. "I don't know anything about cleaning horses. I've never even washed my *dog!* We take him to the Poodle Parlor once a month, and they do everything."

"Well, since we don't have a Horse Parlor, you're just going to have to learn," Pam said. "Emily, how about lending Caro a hand, since you've done such a good job with Joker? And you better step on it—classes start in twenty minutes, and Dad expects everybody to be on time."

"Twenty *minutes?*" Caro groaned. "It'll take twenty *years!*"

Pam grinned. "I doubt it. If you need help saddling up, let me know." She hurried off in response to a call from Penny, and Emily went into Vic's stall. She took the rubber curry comb from Caro and began currying the big bay until all the dried mud was gone. Then she brushed him all over, to remove the dust. Last, she handed a rubbing cloth to Caro, who had been leaning against Vic's feed trough looking bored, and she showed her how to polish the horse's coat until it shone.

"There! Grooming a horse really isn't hard, once you get the hang of it," Emily said, rubbing her dusty hands on her jeans. "Want me to help you with his saddle and bridle?" she asked.

"No, that's okay. I'm not *completely* helpless!" Caro stamped out of the stall and hauled down the English saddle and bridle that hung next to the door. "I can manage just fine."

The other campers were beginning to lead their horses out of the stable to the mounting block in the stable yard. Libby trotted by, leading Foxy, whose gleaming coat and equally gleaming tack showed her competence with her mount. She was beaming when she waved at Emily as she passed. Several Foals followed, holding the reins of their fat little ponies. The Thoros, most of whom had been at Webster's before, were already on their way to the training ring.

Emily quickly tacked up Joker and joined the parade. As she passed Vic's stall, she heard Caro saying, "Horse, *stand still!* How can I fasten the girth if you keep dancing around all the time?"

Emily wondered if she should give Caro a hand, but decided against it. Caro had said she could manage. Well, let her manage then, since she hadn't even bothered to thank Emily for her help in grooming Dark Victory. Emily led Joker to the mounting block and checked the length of his stirrup leathers to make sure they were right for her. Then she swung up into the saddle. As she guided Joker out of the stable yard toward the ring, she began to worry. What if she'd been placed in a beginners' class with a lot of Foals? She would feel pretty silly among a group of little kids, and she bet Joker would feel silly, too, surrounded by a lot of ponies.

But it would be even worse to start out in an intermediate class and have Matt decide she wasn't good enough after all, and make her join the beginners. Then maybe he'd decide she wasn't a good enough rider for Joker, either, and she'd be given another horse. Emily didn't think she could stand it if that happened!

Caro trotted past Emily on Dark Victory. She'd washed off the smudges on her face, and her golden hair—exactly the color of Joker's coat—had been neatly smoothed back into a tight bun. She looked like the girls Emily had seen riding in horse shows, who won blue ribbons in every class. Caro didn't even glance at Emily.

Emily tightened her grip on Joker's reins. Her hands were perspiring, and there was a tight knot in her stomach. If only she wouldn't mess up! If Judy were here, it wouldn't matter so much—they'd both be in the same group, Emily was sure. Caro, Libby, and Lynda would be in the advanced classes. That left Dru, Penny, and Danny.

Just then Emily caught sight of Dru. Her round face was pale, and she was clutching Donna's reins

and trying to hold onto the saddle at the same time. Plump, placid Donna just ambled along calmly, apparently not concerned in the least about her terrified rider. Now *there* was a beginner all right, Emily thought. Poor Dru! Why had she come to Webster's if she was so scared of horses? Penny was riding beside Dru on Dr. Pepper, talking softly to her. Whatever she said seemed to make Dru feel a little better, because Dru gave a small smile. Would Penny be a beginner or an intermediate? Emily wondered. Penny's booted feet were shoved all the way through the stirrups, and she was holding the reins awkwardly, but she didn't look scared.

Danny came up beside Emily, sitting very straight in the saddle, toes up, heels down just the way they were supposed to be. Her dark eyes were shining as she said, "Isn't this great? I can't wait for classes to begin! I'm going to learn absolutely *everything* this summer! Misty's such a neat horse—I hope I don't foul up."

Emily grinned. "Me, too! Maybe we'll be in the same class."

But Danny shook her head. "I doubt it. You look as though you've been riding all your life. I've read dozens of books about riding, but I haven't ridden very much. I bet some of those little kids are better riders than I am."

Looking at several of the Foals, Emily said, "I know what you mean. And I *think* I know what I'm doing, but I've never had a riding lesson in my life.

My friend Judy and I ride at a stable in our home town whenever we get the chance. She was supposed to be here, but she broke her leg, so she couldn't come."

"Oh, is she the one who was going to have the other bunk in our cabin?" Danny asked.

Emily nodded.

"That's tough. I guess you miss her a lot. My best friend, Susan, isn't into horses, so she went to another camp this summer. I thought I was going to be really lonely at Webster's, but now I don't think I will. I just love being here. And I love Misty, too. Maybe next year I'll be able to talk Susan into coming with me."

"Yeah—next year . . ." Emily said. If she didn't mess up, and if she didn't get too homesick, she was sure she'd be coming back next summer, with Judy, just the way they'd planned. Then she'd be one of the old-timers, like Libby and Lynda, and Joker would definitely be her horse, just the way Foxy was Libby's and Dan was Lynda's. She'd show Judy the ropes.

But first, she had to prove that she was worthy of Joker. She kept hearing Caro's words: "What about the palomino? He's the horse I really want." Well, Emily wanted him, too, and she had him. And she was going to keep him, no matter what!

Chapter 6

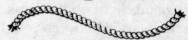

As it turned out, Emily was placed in the intermediate riding class, along with Danny and Penny,
three Foals, and a couple of Thoros. The classes at
Webster's were graded according to ability, not age,
and Emily was surprised to see that there was actually one Thoro in the beginners' ring. Rachel, the
Thoros' counselor, was in charge of the beginners,
Pam instructed the intermediates, and Matt Webster took the advanced riders, one of whom was a
wiry little Foal who couldn't have been more than
ten years old. The horse she was riding was hardly
over fourteen hands high and looked as though it
was mostly mustang, but the girl, whose name Emily
didn't know, handled her mount with practiced
ease.

Pam's voice brought Emily's attention from the
adjoining rings back to her own group.

"The first thing we're going to do is walk—yes, *walk*—our horses all around the ring. It's important for you to get used to the horses you'll be riding for the rest of the summer. You don't know them, and they don't know you. You're going to get acquainted with each other during our first few sessions, and the most important thing is getting to know the feel of your horse as he—or she—gets the feel of you. You're developing a partnership with your horse. You have to learn to trust each other. Backs straight, hands light on the reins, knees tight, heels down, eyes focused between your horse's ears. Emily, lead off."

Emily swallowed hard. She'd hoped to be third or fourth in line, not first, but she clucked softly to Joker, and he started ambling forward. Emily tried to remember everything she'd learned at The Barn. She glanced down at her hands, hoping she was holding the reins properly. She could feel the slight pressure of Joker's mouth. He wasn't pulling or struggling to take a faster pace. With her hands separated evenly across his withers, she concentrated on keeping her legs close without undue pressure, heels down and toes slightly out.

"Good!" Pam said as the last of her students completed the circuit. "Penny, try to keep the balls of your feet in the stirrups. The heels of your boots shouldn't come into contact with the stirrups."

Penny nodded, adjusting the position of her feet.

"Now you're going to trot. Slowly, girls. You're

going to *sit* to this trot, not post. Balance a small part of your weight on the stirrups, keep your hands steady—that's it!"

Joker's slow trot was only slightly faster than his walk. Emily sat tight, rolling with the rhythm of his gait. Her hands remained steady. It was as though she and Joker were one, horse and rider communicating perfectly without words.

When Pam ordered a normal trot, Emily urged Joker into a faster pace. She leaned slightly forward as she raised and lowered her body in time with the beat of his hooves. She'd always wondered why that motion was called "posting"—she'd have to ask Pam about it one of these days.

"Don't jiggle, Danny," Pam called. "Grip with your knees and calves. Try to catch on to his rhythm . . . that's better. Meghan," she said to the only Thoro in the class, "you're hitting the saddle too hard with your rump. Support yourself with your legs. Trotting is supposed to be *fun* for you and the horse, not punishment!"

"I lost my stirrup!" one of the Foals wailed.

"Well, find it again," Pam said cheerfully. "You're not going to fall off . . . there! You did it. Emily, watch those hands—they're wobbling, and your reins are too long."

"Sorry, Joker," Emily muttered as she adjusted her grip. Joker's ears flicked briefly back and forth, as though he accepted her apology.

As the class progressed, Emily discovered that she

was far from the worst rider in her group. She wasn't the best, either—that was probably Meghan—but she wasn't ashamed of herself. And most important of all, she knew she'd learned more about riding in this one morning than she had in all the time she and Judy had been going to The Barn. By the time classes were dismissed so the campers could rub down their mounts and wash up for lunch, she was feeling pretty good about herself.

"It's all because of you," she told Joker as she walked him around the stable yard to cool him down. "You know exactly what to do and where to go—all I have to do is grip with my legs, turn out my toes, and hold the reins!"

"How'd it go, Emily?" Libby asked, pulling Foxy up next to Emily and Joker. She was cooling Foxy by riding him bareback, rather than leading him as the other girls did.

"Terrific!" Emily said happily. "I was sure I was going to slide off when Pam had us do a slow trot with our feet out of the stirrups, but I didn't. We even cantered with no stirrups, and Joker's gait is so smooth that I hardly even bounced."

"You're lucky," Caro said as she came up beside them, pulling Vic's leadline impatiently. "This one trots like he's trying to pound my backbone right into my skull! It's like riding a pile driver."

Libby swung her right leg over Foxy's back so she was sitting sideways. "Vic does have kind of a rough trot," she said. "But you'll get used to it. And wait till we start jumping! Vic's the best jumper Webster's has—except for Foxy," she added, giving her horse a pat. "By the way, Caro, you shouldn't yank on his lead like that. He doesn't like it."

"Well, *I* don't like *him*, so we're even!" Caro grumbled. "I don't think I'll *ever* get used to him."

She stomped off toward the stable, still tugging at Vic's lead. Emily gazed after them, shaking her head in amazement. Imagine not liking a horse—*any* horse! Caroline Lescaux was a very peculiar girl.

She stroked Joker's shoulder and found that he was completely cool and dry. "Okay, fella, you've earned a break," she told him. "And I've earned some lunch—I'm starving!"

As Emily led Joker to his stall, she heard the big bell clanging, calling the campers to their midday meal. In spite of her hunger, she gave the palomino a brisk rubdown and made sure he had plenty of fresh, sweet hay to munch on. Before she left, she put her arms around his neck and nuzzled him affectionately.

"See you soon," she whispered. "And thanks for making me look good out there in the ring!"

After lunch, which the Foals served and the Thoros cleared away, there was a period of "unstructured time" when the campers could do as they pleased—within reason.

"No swimming or boating," Pam told the Fillies. "Water sports come next, at two, and there'll be a lifeguard on duty then. *Nobody* goes in the water without supervision, not even with a buddy, understand? And no riding on your own, either. The summer's just beginning, and we don't want to lose anybody right at the start!"

Everybody nodded. Dru looked worried. "Did you ever? Lose anybody, I mean?" she asked anxiously.

Pam's hearty laugh rang out. "Of course not! I was just teasing, Dru. We take very good care of our campers at Webster's."

Caro peered out the window of the Fillies' cabin. "Where are *they* going?" she asked, referring to several Thoros who were following Rachel, their counselor, to a big, green van parked nearby.

"I guess Rachel's driving them into town," Pam replied.

Caro brightened. "Can I go, too? I'll be bored to tears hanging around here with nothing to do."

"Not today, Caro," Pam said firmly. "Maybe tomorrow after supper we'll all go and check out Skeet's Sugar Shop—they have fantastic homemade ice cream."

"Ice cream?" Dru's round face lit up. "I love ice cream!"

Caro raised one eyebrow. "That's obvious," she said dryly, and Dru blushed.

"Caro . . ." Pam warned, frowning.

"Okay, okay." Caro flopped down on her bunk and began taking off her riding clothes. "If we can't swim, and we can't go into town, I'm going to catch some rays. It's not against the rules to sunbathe, is it?"

Pam just gave her a look, then said, "I'm going up to the house for a while. See you guys at the dock at two."

Danny and Lynda decided to sunbathe with Caro, and Penny and Dru, seated side by side on Dru's bunk, started writing letters home. Emily wanted to finish the letter she'd started to Judy, so when Libby asked if she wanted to go and say hello to the mares and foals, Emily shook her head.

"Maybe later. Thanks anyway," she said, and Libby sprinted out the door.

Four closely written pages later, Emily decided there was only one thing missing from her letter to Judy—a picture of Joker. Pam had said no riding, but surely it would be all right to visit the stable and take a photograph. She took her Polaroid camera out of her trunk, checked to make sure she had several shots left, and headed for the door—on tiptoe, because Penny had climbed up into her own bunk, and she and Dru were both taking naps.

"Where are you going?" Lynda called as Emily passed the three sunbathers.

"To take a picture of my horse," Emily replied, holding up the camera.

Caro sat up, pushing her sunglasses on top of her

head. "Why don't you take a picture of us?" she suggested.

"Oh, no!" Danny wailed. "My hair's a mess, and these shorts make my thighs look humongous!"

"Me, too," Lynda added. "Just take a picture of Caro—she looks terrific."

Emily had to admit that Caro *did* look terrific in her tropical print bikini. But then, Caro looked great in anything. Too bad she wasn't as nice as she was pretty, Emily thought.

"I've got a better idea," Caro said, rising gracefully to her feet. "I'll come to the stable with you, and you can take a picture of me with Joker. Then I'll take a picture of the two of you, okay?"

"Sure," Emily said. "But wouldn't you rather have a picture of yourself with Vic, since he's your horse?"

"No—Joker," Caro said. She put on her sandals. "Let's go!"

Emily hesitated. "I think you ought to wear real shoes," she said. "You might step on a nail or something. Back home at The Barn, where my friend Judy and I ride, they won't even let you into the stable if you're not wearing boots. What if Joker steps on your foot?"

Caro rolled her eyes. "Really! You're as bad as Pam. I'll be perfectly fine. Let's go," she repeated.

Emily shrugged. "All right. Just watch where you step—and where Joker steps!"

Chapter 7

The stable was cool and dim in contrast to the bright, hot afternoon sunlight. Emily and Caro headed for Joker's stall, and he stuck his head out over the door, giving a little whicker of welcome. Beaming, Emily stroked his nose and rested her cheek against his neck. "I think he knows me already," she said happily.

"He probably thinks you brought him a treat," Caro said. Looking around, she frowned. "It's awfully dark in here. We'll never get a decent picture, even with the flash. Let's take him out into the stable yard."

"I don't think we're supposed to—" Emily began, but Caro cut her off.

"There you go again!" she sighed. "Pam said no *riding*. We're not going to be riding—we're just taking pictures. And besides, nobody's around to see us." Swiftly, she unlatched the door, took hold of Joker's halter, and led him out of the stall. Emily followed reluctantly. She had a very strong feeling that they shouldn't be doing this, but it was obvious that once Caro set her mind on something, there was no stopping her.

"Here's a good spot," Caro said as she approached a place where the stable yard fence was overgrown with honeysuckle. "It's the perfect background." She draped one arm around Joker's neck and flashed a dazzling smile. "You can take the picture now."

As Emily pushed the button, she couldn't help thinking that Caro and Joker looked as though they belonged together, sleek and golden as they both were. *But he's not her horse, he's mine,* she told herself.

The camera spat out the print, and both girls watched as the image developed. Emily thought the picture was great, but Caro made a face.

"I look cross-eyed," she said. "Would you mind taking another one, Emily?"

So Emily did, but that one didn't suit Caro either. On the third try, she was finally satisfied, and consented to change places with Emily. But for some reason, the picture she took didn't come out very well. It was a little blurry, and Emily's face was in a shadow.

"Could you take another one?" Emily asked.

Caro checked the counter. "Sorry—that was the

last picture. If you have another pack of film, we can try again tomorrow."

"Hey, what are you doing out here?" said a deep voice from inside the stable. Emily and Caro looked up to see Warren Webster striding over to them. Emily's heart sank, but Caro didn't blink an eye.

"Oh, hi, Warren," she said, her voice as sweet as the honeysuckle on the fence. "Emily wanted me to take a picture of her and Joker. It's all right, isn't it? I mean, we haven't broken any rules or anything, have we?" She fluttered her lashes, and Warren seemed to have lost the power of speech for a moment. Apparently he also thought Caro looked terrific in her bikini.

Finally he said, "Uh . . . well, not exactly. But campers aren't supposed to take horses out unless there's a counselor or somebody around."

"Then it's all right, because *you're* around," Caro said pertly. "Want to see the pictures Emily took of me?" She held out the prints, and Warren looked at them with great interest. "You can keep one if you like," she went on.

"Uh . . . thanks. This one's a real good likeness of Joker," Warren said, tucking a print into his shirt pocket. "You better take him back to his stall now, before Dad finds out."

As Emily led Joker toward the stable, she heard Caro saying, "You won't tell on us, will you? I wouldn't want Emily to get in trouble, just because she bent the rules a little."

Emily's mouth fell open in astonishment. It hadn't been *her* idea to take Joker out of the stable!

"No, I won't tell," Warren said. "But don't do it again. We don't want anybody getting hurt."

He waited while Emily put Joker back into his stall and carefully latched the door. Then he headed for the house as Emily and Caro took off in the direction of the Fillies' bunkhouse. Emily was very annoyed.

"Why did you say that—about me bending the rules?" she asked.

Caro looked at her, surprised. "So you wouldn't get into trouble, like I told Warren."

"But it wasn't *me*—" Emily began.

"Oh, Emily, don't be silly." Caro laughed. "So I should have said 'we.' What does it matter? This isn't a *prison* camp, you know! They won't string you up by your thumbs if you do something just a teeny bit wrong."

"But I didn't—"

"Of course you didn't. And neither did I. I bet I know the *real* reason you're mad."

"I'm not mad, exactly," Emily said. And she wasn't, not exactly. She was getting confused, though. Somehow Caro was making it sound, even to Emily, as if she'd been at fault. And she wasn't—was she?

"Yes, you are. You're mad because I made you use up all your film on Joker and me, and I don't blame you one bit. Tell you what—when we go into town tomorrow night, I'll buy you a whole new pack of film, and I'll take lots of pictures of you. And Joker, of course. I'm really sorry that the one I took today didn't come out, but it's because you turned your head. It wasn't my fault, honest."

"That's okay," Emily assured her. "And you don't have to buy me more film. I should have noticed there were only four shots left." Why was she apologizing to Caro? It should have been the other way around. Emily was becoming more confused by the minute.

"Hey, you two, where have you been? It's almost two o'clock—time for swimming," Lynda shouted as Emily and Caro approached the cabin. She and Danny were wearing their swimsuits and had towels slung around their necks. "Want us to wait for you? Libby's already gone, and so have Penny and Dru."

"No, you go ahead. We'll meet you there," Caro said. She tucked her arm through Emily's, much to Emily's surprise, and whispered in her ear, "That tank suit of Lynda's must've come from the McKay's catalog. It makes her look like that cow she's so proud of!"

"Oh, Caro, that's mean!" Emily whispered back. "I thought Lynda was your friend."

"Well, she's *kind of* my friend," Caro said. "But let's face it—she's a little chunky. Not like you. You've got a really good figure, Emily. You know, I bet you'd look great in a bikini. And I bet you don't own one, right?"

"No, I don't," Emily admitted.

"I have six," Caro told her. "Why don't you borrow one? Take your pick. Really, I mean it. But hurry up—I don't know about you, but I'm absolutely *broiling*!"

Ten minutes later, Emily and Caro were walking down the path that led to the dock. Emily was wearing one of Caro's suits—what there was of it—and she'd wrapped her towel around her waist sarong-fashion to hide her pale tummy. She had never felt so naked in her life. What if the top fell off when she dived into the water? She'd die of embarrassment!

"Hey, Emily, you should've come with me to see the foals!" said Libby as Emily and Caro joined the rest of the campers at the water's edge. Libby's suit was wet and baggy, and her short red hair was plastered to her head. "There are four of them this year, and they're the most adorable things you've ever seen. And there are six lambs in the sheep pasture!"

"I just *love* lamb," Caro said before Emily could say a word. "Lamb chops, leg of lamb, and lots of mint jelly. I'm going down to the water, Emily. Are you coming?"

"In a minute," Emily said. She clutched her towel more tightly around her waist. None of the other Fillies were wearing bikinis, though several of the Thoros were.

"That's a neat suit," Libby said. "At least, the top is." She giggled. "Something the matter with the bottom?"

"Not exactly. It's kind of small, that's all. It's not mine—it's Caro's," Emily told her.

Libby looked surprised, but all she said was, "Oh."

"She has a lot of them, and she practically insisted that I wear one," Emily said. Somehow she felt she was apologizing again.

"Want to swim?" Libby asked. "Race you to the float! But you'll have to drop that towel."

Emily grinned. "Okay, but if the bottom falls off, I'm not coming out till it gets dark!"

With a whoop, Libby charged across the grass, and Emily followed. They zipped past Melinda in the lifeguard's chair and plunged into the water, Emily letting out a squeal at its coldness. But it felt good on her hot skin, and she swam with all her might, trying to catch up with Libby. They reached the float at almost the same moment, sputtering and laughing.

"I won by a nose!" Libby yelled, hauling herself up onto the raft.

"No fair! You had a head start!"

Emily clambered up the ladder and collapsed, glad to see that Caro's bikini was still in place. Caro was on the float, lounging next to Beth and Ellen, two bikini-clad Thoros. Every golden hair on Caro's head was in place—apparently she'd managed to swim out without getting her head wet.

"Doesn't that suit look good on Emily?" she said to the other girls. And to Emily, "See. I told you it

84

wouldn't fall off! It's my suit," she told Beth and Ellen, "but I let Emily wear it because she was so *nice* to me today."

"I was?" Emily blurted, surprised.

"You sure were. You showed me how to groom Vic, and then this afternoon you used up all your film taking pictures of Joker and me." Then to Ellen and Beth—and Libby, because she happened to be there—Caro said, "Emily has this really neat Polaroid camera. If Pam takes us into town tomorrow after supper, I'm going to buy her a new pack of film. Hey, Emily, I think you ought to take pictures of all the Fillies and their horses! We could stick them up on the walls of our cabin, and make it look a little less like an army barrack."

"That's a great idea," Libby said, and Beth added, "How about taking some pictures of the Thoros? We could use some interior decoration, too."

"Okay—why not?" Emily said. The sun beat down on her as she lay between Caro and Libby on the canvas-covered float, and Emily was beginning to feel drowsy. But she was already thinking about what she'd write in her next letter to Judy. She'd been pretty hard on Caro in the letter she'd finished earlier. Perhaps she hadn't really been fair. Caro certainly seemed to be trying to make up for her nasty behavior. And it wasn't her fault that her parents were wealthy and spoiled her a lot . . . Emily thought as she dozed off.

*   *   *

Later that afternoon, the Foals, Fillies, and Thoros gathered at the stables to saddle up their mounts again. Their counselors led them on a tour of the Webster farm, past fields where corn was beginning to tassel and squash was ripening on the vines, through the apple orchard, and then along the river and through the woods to a pasture where several mares were grazing while their foals cavorted around them. Emily could hardly tear herself away—the foals, only three months old, were the cutest things she'd ever seen. The next time Libby went to visit them, she'd be sure to go along.

Then they stopped by the sheep meadow. The lambs looked like animated stuffed toys, frisking on spindly little legs. The girls all oohed and aahed, and even Dru smiled as she watched them.

"They're so little and cuddly," she said to Emily. "I never saw a real live lamb up close before. Are we allowed to pet them, or would their mothers get mad?"

"You can pet them if you can catch them," Libby said with a grin. "Those little guys are pretty fast on their feet! I walked over here after lunch today. You should have come with me, Dru."

"You didn't ask me," Dru pointed out shyly.

"Uh . . . no, I guess I didn't. Sorry about that. Next time, I'll let you know, okay?"

Dru nodded, and Penny asked, "Me, too?"

"Sure, why not?"

Emily noticed that for the first time, Dru looked

really happy. For a few minutes she even forgot to hang onto her saddle.

"The Websters sell their wool to people who make beautiful sweaters," Libby added. "But Marie keeps some to make sweaters for the family. She cards and spins and knits it all by hand."

"My mother made me a sweater for Christmas," Penny said. "I brought it with me to camp, just in case it gets cold."

"Come on, Fillies," Pam called. "Time to get moving!"

When they had made a circuit of the entire farm, the campers rubbed down their horses, watered them, and led them to the pasture where they would spend the night. As she gave Joker an affectionate pat and watched him trot off, Emily said, "I wish we could sleep out here, too."

"Libby did once," Lynda said. "She sneaked out one night last year with a sleeping bag after lights out. Boy, did Pam blow her stack!"

"I'd be scared," Dru said.

"Me, too," Penny added.

"I wouldn't be scared, but I can't imagine why anyone would want to," Caro said with a shudder. "You'd be eaten alive by mosquitoes, and a horse would probably step on your head!"

"When is the first overnight trail ride?" Emily asked. "I can't wait to camp out with Joker."

Pam joined them just then. "Not until next week—Thursday, if it doesn't rain. Okay, Fillies, time to wash up. It's our turn to set the tables for supper, so I'll see you up at the house in fifteen minutes."

Emily lingered behind as the rest of the girls started for the cabin. Folding her arms on the top rail of the fence, she gazed dreamily at Joker. Her legs ached from so much riding, and she'd probably be stiff as a board in the morning, but she didn't care. All she needed to be perfectly content right now was Judy—but Emily realized, with a little stab of guilt, that she wasn't missing her best friend nearly as much as she'd thought she would.

Chapter 8

Emily was sure Caro would either forget or change her mind about buying film for Emily's camera, and she almost wished she would. Those film packs were expensive, and though she knew Caro could afford it, she didn't like the idea of being in Caro's debt. But Caro was as good as her word—even better. The following evening, when Pam took the Fillies into Winnepac, Caro immediately headed for the general store and bought not one, but two packs of film.

"Here. Now I can take lots of pictures of you and Joker, and you'll still have plenty of film left for the rest of the Fillies and the Thoros," she said, thrusting the bag into Emily's hands.

"Thanks, Caro. But you really shouldn't have," Emily said lamely.

"Oh, don't be silly!" Caro gave her one of her

dazzling smiles. "What are friends for, anyway? And we're friends, aren't we?"

"Oh, yes. Sure we are. But I'd feel better if you'd let me pay you back."

"If it'll make you happy, you can pay me back some other time, okay? Now let's catch up with the rest of the gang—Pam said we should meet them at Skeet's, and I'm absolutely *dying* for homemade ice cream! Come on, let's run!"

Caro grabbed Emily's hand, and they ran down Main Street to the brightly lighted sign that proclaimed Skeet's Sugar Shop. They were breathless and laughing as they burst into the ice cream parlor, where Pam, Libby, Lynda, Danny, Penny, and Dru had already pushed three tables together and were trying to decide on ice cream flavors. Emily and Caro took the two vacant chairs, and Emily promptly ordered maple walnut. Caro decided on pistachio. When Dru ordered a banana split, Caro didn't say a word; she just raised her eyebrows as the overflowing dish was set in front of Dru. But as the plump girl dug into the first of three scoops of ice cream, Caro whispered to Emily, "I really feel sorry for Donna. That poor little mare is going to be carrying an extra load tomorrow!"

Emily couldn't help herself—she giggled. And the maple walnut ice cream was the best she'd ever tasted.

Suddenly Caro peered through the plate glass

window and said, "Pam, isn't that your brother Warren walking down the street?"

"Probably," Pam said. "He plays lead guitar in the River Rats, a local rock band. They practice a couple of times a week."

"A rock band? In *Winnepac?*" Caro was astonished. "Where do they play?"

"At the American Legion Hall. There's a dance once a month. Melinda is the Rats' lead vocalist," Pam told her. "She's pretty good, too."

"Can we go?" Caro asked eagerly. "It sounds like fun."

Pam poked at what was left of her ice cream. "The Thoros go sometimes, if Rachel's free to take them."

"What about the Fillies? I'd love to go—wouldn't you, Danny?"

Danny grinned. "It would be neat. I love rock music."

"So do I," Lynda said.

"Then why can't we go to their next gig?" Caro persisted. "Lynda, Danny, Emily, and me. What about it, Pam?"

"I don't know. We'll have to see."

Emily was surprised that Caro had included her. She was even more surprised when their waitress brought the check and Caro insisted on paying for Emily's ice cream, as well as her own. When she protested, Caro just said, "Don't worry about it. You can pay me back later."

"Looks like Caro's turning over a new leaf," Libby said to Emily as they left Skeet's and headed for the van.

"She's been really friendly today," Emily agreed. "I guess Caro's okay."

But she couldn't help thinking: *first the bikini, then the film, now the ice cream.* Emily's debts were mounting up, and she was beginning to feel a little uncomfortable about it.

The rest of the week flew by so quickly that Emily sometimes forgot which day it was. There was always something exciting and interesting to do—riding classes every morning, and water sports (not just swimming, but canoeing, rowing, and even sailing) or volleyball or soccer after lunch. Then more riding in the afternoon, and a campfire or other entertainment each evening.

Even the chores were fun, Emily discovered. She'd lived all her life in a small town and had never spent any time on a farm, unless you counted the Jordans' apple-picking excursions every October to Myers' Farm, where they would spend an afternoon filling plastic bags with juicy, red apples.

At Webster's, the campers cared for their horses, and Emily didn't consider that a chore at all. She loved grooming Joker, rubbing neat's-foot oil into his saddle to keep the leather soft, and even cleaning out his stall.

The campers also helped Marie in the kitchen.

They set and cleared the tables and picked fresh vegetables for supper. When the Fillies had garden detail, Pam always put Lynda in charge, since Lynda had been born and raised on her family's farm.

"Bet you thought lettuce grows in plastic bags, the way you see it in the supermarket," Lynda said on the Fillies' first trip to the vegetable garden. "Well, it doesn't. My mom says that stuff isn't fit for the hogs—our hogs eat real well," she added proudly.

"I really don't care what your hogs eat," Caro sighed. "Could we just get this over with? Show me what to pick and I'll pick it." She bent down and pulled off a handful of dark, bushy greens before Lynda could reply.

Lynda giggled. "I don't think Marie will be too happy if you bring her that," she said. "It's a weed! The lettuce is over here, the ruffly green stuff with reddish edges. Here—you and Danny can start filling this basket."

"How was I supposed to know?" Caro tossed the weed away. Ignoring Danny, she said to Emily, "Come on, Emily. *You* help me pick this stuff, okay?"

Libby looked up from where she was kneeling, pulling radishes, and raised her eyebrows, but for once she didn't say anything. Emily could tell that she was wondering why Caro kept seeking Emily out. Emily couldn't help wondering, too. She didn't worry about it, though. She was just glad Caro was being pleasant for a change.

"When we have enough lettuce for the salad, let's thin out some of those carrots," she suggested to Caro. "Lynda said there are too many of them, and we can give the ones we pull to our horses."

"Okay," Caro said. "I bet Joker will just love them."

"So will Vic," Emily reminded her.

Caro shrugged. "I guess . . ."

Emily decided she'd save her carrots to give Joker the next day, when she paid her usual early-morning visit to the pasture where the horses spent the night. She was always the first Filly to wake up each morning, and before the rest of the girls opened their eyes, Emily put on her riding clothes and made a beeline for the pasture. She'd climb the fence and whistle the way Eric had taught her—long and low, but piercing—and wherever Joker happened to be, he'd hear her and amble over. His golden coat would be damp with dew, and he'd smell wonderful, like horse, and grass, and something else that Emily couldn't quite identify. She secretly imagined it must be moonlight, though she knew perfectly well that moonlight didn't have a smell.

Then she would give him handfuls of honeysuckle and sweet clover that she'd picked on the way. Tomorrow morning she'd give him tiny young carrots as well. Then she'd kiss his nose and hurry back, just in time for breakfast. Pam didn't object to Emily's early-morning visits. There were no camp rules against spending free time with your horse, as long

as you didn't ride him without supervision. And Emily never did. She just loved being alone with him, without all the other girls around—especially Caro.

Sometimes it seemed to Emily that Caro was acting *too* friendly. Emily would have liked to spend more time with Libby, but Caro didn't like the mischievous little redhead, and Libby didn't like Caro, either. Caro didn't seem to like any of the Fillies much, except Emily.

The day after the Fillies' trip into Winnepac, Caro had insisted that Emily try on a pair of her European stretch riding pants. Though Emily protested, she told her to keep them because they fit so well. Emily didn't want to hurt her feelings, so she wore them to her next riding class. After all, Joker deserved to have a rider who looked as elegant as he himself did, and Emily felt *very* elegant in a pair of pants that had probably cost as much as her entire wardrobe.

Then there was the River Rats' gig at the American Legion Hall. They were playing on Friday night, which was the same night as the first hayride of the season. Emily had really been looking forward to the hayride.

"It's super fun," Libby told her. "Matt hitches the tractor to this gigantic wagon filled with hay, and we go all over the place! It's so neat—we sing and yell and all that stuff, and when we get back, Marie always has ice-cold lemonade and popcorn absolutely *dripping* with butter. You'll love it, Emily."

"You'll hate it, Emily," Caro said the minute she got Emily alone. They were saddling up their horses for the afternoon ride. "It's only Fillies and Foals. The Thoros are all going into town to hear the River Rats, and I'm going, too. Pam said it was okay. Come with us, Emily. You don't really want to bounce around in a hay wagon with all those little Foals, do you?"

"Well—" Emily began, but Caro cut her off.

"Of course you don't. You're not a silly little kid, not like the rest of the Fillies."

"What about Danny?" Emily asked. "And Lynda? Don't they want to go?"

"Who cares?" Caro tossed her lovely golden head. "I want *you* to come with me."

"But I don't have anything to wear. . . ." Emily mumbled.

"No problem. You can wear something of mine. And I'll pay for your admission, too."

"Caro, I can pay! I really can. But I think I'd like to go on the hayride—"

"No, you wouldn't. Okay, I won't pay for your admission. But I have this absolutely *fabulous* tank top that will look great on you. I'll lend you a scarf and some jewelry, too. You're coming, Emily, and you're going to have a *wonderful* time!"

So Emily went. It was kind of fun to be part of the older crowd, but as Rachel headed the green van down the road toward Winnepac, Emily saw the

Foals and the rest of the Fillies piling into the big hay wagon, and she wished she could be in two places at once. She'd never gone on a hayride before, and she knew there wouldn't be another one for several weeks. But she'd never been to a rock concert, either, and the River Rats wouldn't be playing again until next month. Emily wondered what Judy would have done in her place. Somehow, she was pretty sure Judy would have chosen the hayride.

"I can hardly wait to hear the Rats play, can you?" Meghan asked. She looked very different from her usual self tonight. Her short, dark hair stood up in jagged spikes on top of her head, and she was wearing big, dangling earrings and lots of eye makeup. All the Thoros, and especially Caro, had dressed and made themselves up to look as exotic as possible. Even Emily hardly recognized herself when she looked in the mirror. Emily never wore makeup, except for an occasional touch of lip gloss, and now she felt as if she had on a mask. Caro had insisted on making her up, using her own eye shadow, eye liner, lipstick, and blusher. Emily had to admit it made her look much older, but it was also making her skin itch, particularly around the eyes, and she didn't dare rub or scratch her face for fear of ruining Caro's handiwork.

"Nobody would ever guess that you're only thirteen," Caro had said, standing back to admire the effect. "I just *knew* my black top would fit you perfectly, and that bandanna matches the turquoise in my bracelet. Too bad your ears aren't pierced, or you could have worn my silver Navaho earrings, too."

Caro herself was dressed all in white—white slacks, white midriff top, white sandals, and a white scarf tied around the golden pony tail that jutted at a rakish angle from the top of her head. Emily thought *she* looked at least *seventeen.*

"Warren had a different band last summer," Lisa said. "It was called Nightcrawler, if you can believe it! They were pretty good. Are any of the same guys in the River Rats?" she asked Rachel.

"Are any of them as cute as Warren?" Caro added with a giggle.

"I don't know who's in the Rats," Rachel replied. "As for cute, you'll have to decide for yourself. And don't forget, Caro, Warren is Melinda's boyfriend."

"Well, there's no harm in *looking,"* Caro said, tossing her ponytail.

"I wonder if any of the Long Branch boys will be there," Ellen remarked.

Rachel sighed. "Don't you girls ever think about anything except boys?"

"Horses!" Beth called from the back of the van, and everybody laughed. Emily laughed, too, but she didn't really see what was so funny. She hardly ever thought about boys, but she thought about horses all the time.

Rachel found a parking place around the corner from the American Legion Hall, and the girls hurried toward the entrance. Emily was surprised at how many young people were thronging through the doors—it looked like every teenager in Winnepac had come to hear the Rats. When Emily opened her wallet to pay for her admission, Caro shook her head. "I'll take care of it," she said. "You can pay me back later." She also paid for Emily's soda, and wouldn't take the money Emily tried to give her. "Later," she said, giving Emily a big, warm smile. "Don't worry about it, Emily. Look—the guys are coming out!"

"So's Melinda," Ellen said.

Caro gave a little sniff. "Well, she's very pretty, if you like that type. But I wonder how good a singer she is."

Melinda turned out to be a very good singer indeed, and everybody said the Rats were super. Emily guessed they were—she didn't know much about rock bands—but they certainly were *loud*. The whole place seemed to throb and pound with the beat of the music, and so did Emily's head after about half an hour.

"Isn't this fun?" Caro shouted in her ear, and Emily nodded and smiled, wondering how much more "fun" she'd be able to stand. The crowded hall was hot and stuffy. Emily sipped at her soda, and Beth, who was sitting next to her, bumped Emily's elbow just as she was taking a swallow. The soda went down the wrong way, and to her dismay, Emily began to hiccup. She hated getting the hiccups, and once she got started, it seemed as if she'd never stop.

Emily hiccuped as quietly as possible for the rest of the evening. By the time the hiccups let up, the concert was over and the audience had poured out into the street. By then, she was feeling sick to her stomach. Her head ached, her eyes were itching, and all she wanted to do was curl up in a quiet corner somewhere and go to sleep. As Emily climbed into the van, the other girls were chattering excitedly.

"Wasn't it terrific?"

"Wasn't Warren great?"

"I thought the drummer was adorable."

"Melinda wasn't all that good."

"Oh, Caro, you're just jealous!"

"When's their next gig? Not until next *month?*"

"I *told* you you'd have a wonderful time!" Caro said, squeezing into the seat next to Emily, but Emily didn't reply—she felt much too groggy. Her last coherent thought before she dozed off was of how much she owed Caro. The bikini, the film, the ice cream, the riding pants, the clothes and jewelry she'd worn tonight, the admission fee to see the River Rats, the soda . . . how would she ever be able to pay Caro back?

Chapter 9

"You really look good out there on Joker," Caro said on Saturday morning. She'd stopped by the intermediate training ring after her own classes were over, and now she fell into step beside Emily as she walked Joker around the stable yard. "You're doing a lot better than I am! Vic and I don't seem to be on the same wavelength. I mean, he's okay, I guess, but he's kind of *boring*. I think maybe they made a mistake when they assigned Vic to me. Pam said he was hard to handle—well, he's not. I bet you could ride him every bit as well as I do, maybe better."

Emily was pleased that Caro thought she was riding well. "Thanks, Caro. But Vic's not my horse, he's yours," she said, stroking Joker's silky neck.

"That's only because Matt thinks Vic's a handful, and he really isn't." Caro sighed. "I honestly think he's wrong. Joker's every bit as spirited as Vic." She

103

reached out and stroked the palomino, too. Suddenly she said, "Hey, Emily, I have a great idea! Let's switch horses!"

Emily stopped in her tracks, jerking on the reins so hard that Joker gave her a reproachful look.

"Switch horses?" she echoed. "You want me to trade *Joker* for *Vic?*"

"Oh, not forever, silly," Caro said, laughing. "Don't look so horrified. I mean this afternoon, when we go on the trail ride along the river. It'll be fun. Pam won't mind—she knows what a good rider you are. And Matt won't mind, either, if we tell him we both agree. And we *do* agree, don't we, Emily? We're friends, aren't we? And friends share things, don't they? I mean, I've shared lots of things with you. So share Joker with me, just for this afternoon, okay?"

When Caro put it that way, it was hard for Emily to think of a reason to refuse. Still, the thought of letting anybody else ride her beloved Joker, even for a few hours, was upsetting to her. She gently pulled on his reins and continued toward the stable with Caro at her side.

It was true—she owed Caro a lot, and she hadn't paid her back. Caro wouldn't let her. Emily had figured out exactly how much money she owed for the two packs of Polaroid film, the ice cream, the River Rats concert, and the soda—thirty dollars and seventy-four cents—and she had tried to give it to Caro before breakfast, but Caro had refused to take it, saying, as she always did, that Emily could pay her back later. She wouldn't take back the clothing and jewelry she'd loaned Emily, either. So if she wanted to ride Joker just this once, the least Emily could do was agree to trade.

"Come on, Emily," Caro said now. "What's the big deal? You ride Vic this afternoon, and I ride Joker. I'm not going to *hurt* him or anything, for goodness sake!"

"Well . . . okay," Emily said at last. What harm could it possibly do? And as Caro had pointed out, friends are supposed to share.

"Great!" Caro gave Emily a hug, then sprinted off in the direction of the cabin. "I'll tell Pam. You don't have to worry about a thing!" she called over her shoulder.

Emily stared after her for a moment, lost in thought. When Joker nudged her with his nose, she led him into the stable to remove his saddle and bridle, and give him a rubdown before lunch. The Fillies were on dish detail today, so she didn't have to show up early to set the tables.

But after she'd rubbed Joker down and fastened his stall door, she happened to glance into Vic's stall. The big bay's dark coat was dull, and where his saddle had been, there was a darker patch, showing that Caro hadn't cooled him down or rubbed and curried him. Emily hesitated for a moment—after all, Vic was Caro's horse, not hers—but then she slipped into his stall. If she was going to ride him this afternoon, he was kind of her responsibility as well. She gave him a quick rubdown, then patted him and hurried out of his stall just as she heard the big bell ringing to call all the campers to lunch. She almost ran into Libby, who was also racing for the farmhouse.

"What were you doing in Vic's stall?" Libby asked as the two girls ran out of the stable yard. "Is Caro turning you into her stable hand?"

"No. I just wanted to help her out a little. I guess she forgot to cool Vic down after class," Emily said. "And since I'm going to be riding him this afternoon . . ."

"How come?"

"Uh . . . well, we decided to trade horses for the trail ride," Emily said.

Libby's sparkling hazel eyes narrowed. "How'd she sucker you into that? Emily, like my grandmother says, give some people an inch and they'll take a mile." She slowed her pace and faced Emily. "Caro wants Joker—and not just for the trail ride, but for the whole summer. You better watch out. If you let her ride Joker this afternoon, next thing you know she'll snatch him right out from under you!"

Emily took off her hard hat and brushed her damp hair out of her eyes. "It's not that way at all," she protested. "Caro's my friend. She wouldn't do something like that to me."

"Wanna bet? Caro's used to getting what she

106

wants, and she wants Joker more than she wants you for a friend."

That hurt. Emily began jogging again, but Libby kept pace with her.

"Listen, don't be mad at me, okay? I'm your friend too, remember," Libby said. "Hey, maybe I'm wrong. Maybe Caro really *is* Miss Sweetness. But I don't trust her. I think she's Miss Spoiled."

Emily didn't reply—she couldn't. She was too out of breath from running up the hill. The minute the girls burst into the dining hall, Caro, all smiles, waved at Emily.

"Emily, over here!" she called. "I saved you a seat."

As Emily slipped into a chair between Caro and Beth, she put Libby's warning out of her mind. And when Caro offered to teach her how to handle a Sunfish during water sports that afternoon, she was more than happy to agree.

Since Pam had a dentist appointment in Winnepac during the afternoon riding lesson, Warren Webster, on Led Zeppelin, his big sorrel gelding, was in charge of the Fillies' trail ride. Caro was delighted, and promptly trotted Joker up beside him. Emily, close behind on Dark Victory, couldn't help admiring what a beautiful picture the golden girl and the golden horse made. Caro was wearing a pale yellow polo shirt and fawn-colored stretch riding pants, and her long, blond hair was tied back into a silky ponytail that flowed down her back from under her brown velvet hard hat. Joker pranced and tossed his head, which Emily had learned meant there was too much pressure on the reins—he had a very tender mouth. She wanted to say something about it to Caro, but Caro was talking nonstop to Warren, and besides, Emily was having problems with Vic. He was one of those horses who wasn't happy unless he was in the lead, and he kept trying to get ahead of Joker and Zepp, so Emily had her hands full.

"My friend Emily and I heard your band play the other night," Caro was saying. "We thought you were terrific, didn't we, Emily?"

"Yes, terrific," Emily mumbled, pulling back on the reins. "Vic, *behave*—you're pulling my arms right out of their sockets!"

Caro looked back over her shoulder. "You're doing just fine, Emily. I told you you could handle Vic. Wasn't it nice of Emily to let me ride Joker today, Warren? I've been wanting to ride him from the very first minute I saw him. . . ."

Caro chattered merrily on, and the other Fillies laughed and talked as they followed the narrow trail by the river. Even Penny and Dru had something to say, but Emily was concentrating so hard on keeping Vic in line that she couldn't relax and enjoy the beautiful scenery. By the time they returned to the stable, her arms and back were aching, and Vic's dark coat was almost black with sweat.

When she finally got him cooled down, put away his tack, and gave both Vic and Joker some carrots she'd saved for them, the rest of the girls had finished their stable chores and were on their way to pick vegetables for supper. Emily lingered a moment longer with Joker, checking to make sure that Caro had cared for him properly. Then she sneaked him an extra carrot, gave him a hug, and hurried off to join the other Fillies.

But Caro wasn't there, and when Emily asked Lynda where she was, Lynda just shrugged and said she didn't know. Caro didn't show up at the cabin when everyone was washing up for supper, either.

"I saw her going up to the house right after the trail ride," Danny told her. "Maybe she had another one of her headaches and went to see Marie."

If Caro had a headache, she was apparently over it by suppertime, because Emily saw her talking and giggling with Ellen, Beth, Meghan, and Lisa at one of the tables in the dining hall. This time she hadn't saved a seat for Emily, so Emily sat with the rest of the Fillies. Caro didn't look around for her, and when Emily happened to catch her eye and smiled, Caro glanced quickly away, almost as if she were embarrassed about something. What was the matter with her, anyway? Emily wondered.

Chapter 10

After the delicious brownies that Marie and the Foals had baked for dessert, Matt made a few announcements, and then the Thoros began to clear the tables. Emily was surprised to see that Caro immediately took a trayful of dishes into the kitchen, rather than joining the Fillies as they left the dining room. It certainly looked as if Caro was avoiding her, and Emily wondered why.

She was on her way to the door with Libby and Danny when Matt came over to her.

"Got a minute, Emily?" he asked.

Emily blinked in surprise. "Why . . . sure. Is something wrong?"

Matt smiled. "I hope not," he said, and Emily began to feel uneasy. "Let's go into my office, where we can talk," he continued.

"We're going to the camp store to buy post-cards," Libby said. "Catch you later, Emily, okay?"

Emily nodded. Matt put his arm around her shoulders and Emily walked stiffly beside him, wondering why he wanted to talk to her. Had she broken any rules? Had she done something wrong? She couldn't think of anything, but maybe she'd done something she didn't *know* was wrong. Even worse, what if something was wrong at home? Parents were asked not to call campers during the day unless there was an emergency. Had her mother or father called to say that the house had burned down, or one of them was sick, and Matt wanted to break the news to her gently?

By the time they were inside Matt's cluttered little office, Emily was really worried. She didn't even notice the pictures of horses and the ribbons hanging on the knotty pine walls, or the silver trophies that stood on the shelves. When Matt offered her a chair, she sat on the edge of it, her hands clasped tightly in her lap. Matt pulled up a chair next to hers, rather than sitting behind his desk, and he smiled at her.

"Don't look so nervous, Emily," he said. "You haven't been called into the principal's office for a reprimand, you know."

"My folks . . . there's nothing wrong at home, is there?" Emily asked anxiously.

"Is that what you were thinking? No, Emily, nothing like that."

Emily relaxed a little, but she was still puzzled. "Then, what . . . ?"

"I know you've only been here less than a week," Matt began, "but Marie and I hope you like what you've seen of Webster's so far."

"Oh, yes! It's great," Emily said quickly. "Maybe Marie told you I was kind of homesick at first, but I'm all over that now."

"Glad to hear it. But I understand there's one problem, and that's what I want to talk to you about."

"Problem? I don't—"

"Emily, we know that the most important thing to a girl at Webster's is her horse, and we try to make sure that each girl is happy with her mount. It doesn't always work out, however, and sometimes we decide to assign a different horse to a camper, if we feel it's appropriate."

Emily stared at him, and her heart sank. Was he talking about Joker? Was he going to take Joker away from her?

"I had a talk with Caroline Lescaux today, after the Fillies' trail ride," Matt went on. "She tells me she doesn't really like Dark Victory very much, and she'd like to trade horses with you. Because you've become such close friends, she tells me you don't mind exchanging Joker for Vic. What I want to know, Emily, is *do* you mind? More to the point, is this what you really want? If it is, if you and Caroline agree, I have no objection. Warren said you handled Vic very well today."

Emily finally found her voice, though it sounded more like a squeak. "We agreed to trade, but only for this afternoon. I *love* Joker! I'd rather *die* than give him up!"

Matt nodded, frowning a little. "I see. I wonder why she told me you'd be willing to trade for the rest of the summer?"

All of a sudden, Emily knew. And she also knew why Caro hadn't been able to look her in the eye this evening after talking to Matt. "Because . . . because I *owe* her!" Emily cried. "And she wouldn't let me pay her back." In a rush, she told Matt about the film, the ice cream, the ticket to the River Rats concert, even the soda. "I owe her thirty dollars and seventy-four cents," she said miserably. "And she keeps lending me clothes, too. Expensive clothes. I owe her a lot, so I guess she figures I can pay her back by letting her have Joker."

"I see," Matt said again. "You know, Emily, Joker's worth a lot more than thirty dollars and seventy-four cents—I don't think we have to include the clothes in the grand total."

"Oh, I know that! Joker is, well, he's priceless," Emily murmured. She looked up at Matt, trying very hard not to let the tears in her eyes spill over.

"Do you have the money to pay Caroline back?" Matt asked gently.

"Yes, I do. Even the seventy-four cents."

114

"Then I think you ought to give it to Caroline right away, and if she still refuses to take it, you bring it to Marie or to me, and we'll keep it for her, kind of like a bank, okay?"

Emily nodded. "Okay. But, Matt, what about Joker? Do I have to trade him for Vic? I mean, Vic's a perfectly nice horse, though he pulls a lot, and I love all horses, I really do, but . . ."

"But you love Joker best," Matt finished for her. "No, Emily, Joker's your horse for the summer." He stood up, and Emily did, too, beaming with delight and relief. "And now I think I'll track Caroline down and have another little talk with her."

"What . . . what are you going to say to her?" Emily asked.

"I'm just going to tell her what you told me—that there's been a misunderstanding, and that you don't want to trade," Matt said as they left the office.

"I have a feeling that when you do, Caro's not going to want to be my friend anymore," Emily said softly.

Matt put a hand on her shoulder. "Will that make you very unhappy?" he asked.

"Not nearly as unhappy as losing Joker!" Emily told him. "Besides, I guess if she stops being my friend because she can't have my horse, maybe she wasn't really my friend in the first place."

Matt smiled at her. "You know, Emily, you're a pretty smart Filly. It sounds to me as if Caroline was

115

trying to *buy* your friendship. And real friendship can't be bought, you know."

"Yes, I know." Emily thought about Judy, and Libby, too. "Thanks, Matt. Thanks for everything! Is it all right if I go see Joker now, to tell him he's really mine?" she asked. She felt herself blushing. "I guess that sounds kind of silly, but I talk to him a lot," she added.

"Sounds sensible to me," Matt told her with a grin. "See you at the campfire in a little while. The Foals are putting on some skits, and then the Thoros are going to tell ghost stories, I believe."

"Great!" Emily dashed off happily, but instead of going directly to Joker, she stopped by the cabin, took the thirty dollars and seventy-four cents she'd tucked away in an envelope, and put it under Caro's pillow. Nobody was there but Penny and Dru, who were sitting on the floor playing a game of Monopoly. Emily was glad. She wasn't looking forward to facing Caro at the moment, though she knew it would be even harder after Caro heard what Matt had to say.

"Fine friend *you* turned out to be!"

Caro appeared in the twilight with her hands on her hips, blocking Emily's path as Emily returned from her visit to Joker.

Emily said quietly, "Caro, I'm sorry, but I just don't want to give Joker up. I would have told you myself if you'd asked me, but you didn't."

116

"After all the favors I've done for you, I was *sure* you'd see that you owe me something in return," Caro snapped. "Boy, was I ever wrong! Some people are just ingrates, that's all!"

Keeping her temper with difficulty, Emily said, "I put the money I owe you under your pillow—all of it. And I'll give you back the bikini, and the riding pants, and the boots, and the tank top, and all the rest of your stuff. But I *won't* give up Joker. I love him too much."

Caro scowled. "I was really wrong about you, Emily Jordan. I thought you were such a nice person, but you're not. You're selfish and mean!"

No matter how hard she tried, Emily just couldn't restrain her anger any longer. "Maybe you're right," she said. "Maybe I *am* selfish and mean, but at least I'm not a sneak! I don't go saying things behind people's backs that aren't true!"

Caro avoided Emily's eyes. "I don't know what you're talking about," she said uncomfortably. "We agreed to trade horses. You know we did."

"For the trail ride! But that's not what you told Matt. You told him that I didn't mind letting you have Joker for the rest of the summer! If we're supposed to be such good friends, how come you tried to take Joker away from me?"

"Oh, good grief!" Caro sighed. "So I bent the truth a little. I don't see why you have to make such a big deal out of it."

"It *is* a big deal—to me, anyway," Emily said. "Friends don't do things like that to each other."

There was a long silence, broken only by the chirping of the crickets, and Caro stared down at the ground, scuffing the pine needles underfoot with the toe of one sandal. When she finally spoke, Emily could hardly hear her.

"I don't have very many friends. I'm sorry, okay?"

Surprised and pleased, Emily smiled. "Okay." Maybe Caro wasn't really so bad after all. . . .

Suddenly Caro looked up, tossed her head, and said loudly, "When you give me back my things, make sure you don't forget the bandanna I let you wear to the River Rats gig, and that silver bracelet with the turquoise—it's very valuable, not like the junk the other girls have. And don't expect to keep hanging out with the Thoros and me anymore, either! You're really much too *immature!*"

She turned on her heel and flounced off, the full skirt of her blue print sundress swirling around her long, tanned legs.

Emily stared after her and swallowed hard. Nobody had ever spoken to her like that before, and it made her feel kind of sad and sick inside. Maybe she'd feel better if she wrote all about it to Judy—there was still time before the campfire. She started trudging toward the bunkhouse, and suddenly shrieked as a small figure dropped down beside her from the low-hanging branch of a tree.

"Didn't mean to scare you," Libby said cheerfully,

"but I couldn't help overhearing. That Caro is something else!"

"Yes, she sure is," Emily agreed, once she'd gotten her breath back. "She's something else, all right—something else than my friend, that's for sure!"

"Guess I shouldn't say it, but I will anyway. I told you so," Libby said. "But I have to hand it to you, Emily, you really stood up to her. I knew Caro would try something like this sooner or later, and I kind of thought you'd let her get away with it, but you didn't."

"I'm not very good at fighting," Emily said, "but then I guess I never had anything worth fighting for until Joker."

"He's worth fighting for, all right. And so's Foxy. I'd never let anyone take him away from me!" Libby grinned at Emily. "Want to see something neat?"

"What?" Emily asked.

Libby took a small box from the pocket of her camp shorts and opened the lid just a little, but it was getting so dark that Emily couldn't see inside.

"What is it?" she asked, puzzled.

"It's a huge, terrifically ugly, crawly kind of bug! I found it in the tree just now."

Emily drew back. "I'm not crazy about ugly, crawly bugs," she admitted. "What're you going to do with it?"

Libby's grin was full of mischief. "Oh, I don't know. I thought maybe it would like to take a nice,

long nap in somebody's bunk—somebody like Caro, for instance. Remember how she screamed the night she found the frog?"

Now Emily grinned, too. "That's a really *nasty* idea, Libby," she said admiringly. "Need any help?"

"You bet! Right after campfire tonight, we'll run back to the cabin before the rest of them get there. You can keep watch, and I'll stick it between Caro's sheets."

"I have a better idea," Emily said. *"You* keep watch, and *I'll* put the bug in Caro's bunk. I owe her a favor after all she's done for me!"

Giggling, the two girls raced side by side up the hill.

Emily is having the best summer of her life at Webster's Country Horse Camp, and so are the other campers—except for sad, awkward Dru, who always seems to spoil the fun. She even ruins the girls' first overnight trail ride. Emily tries to be Dru's friend, but nothing seems to work. Then Dru runs away. Now it's up to Emily to find her—and come up with a plan to help Dru have one terrific summer!

Don't miss HORSE CRAZY #2
Happy Trails by Virginia Vail

Virginia Vail is a pseudonym for the author of over a dozen young-adult novels, most recently the ANIMAL INN series. She is the mother of two grown children, both of whom are animal lovers, and lives in Forest Hills, New York with one fat gray cat. Many years ago, Virginia Vail fell in love with a beautiful palomino named Joker. She always wanted to put him in a book. Now she has.